GRIM'S LITTLE REAPER
A CLUB APOCALYPSE NOVELLA

RAISA GREYWOOD

First published under the same title in Dirty Daddies 2021 Anniversary Anthology.

Cover art: Wicked Smart Designs
Editing: Amy Briggs

1

ZACH

"Let me get this straight. You four miscreants are opening a BDSM resort together? And you want me to come to the middle of nowhere, Winslow, Arizona?"

"Yes, sir. We're calling it Club Apocalypse."

"Of course. What else would it be? And stop calling me sir."

Retirement was the devil, Captain Zach Stratton decided. He was actually considering the invitation out of sheer boredom. If nothing else, it would be good to see the Horsemen again.

Although Zach had been their commanding officer, Mark Luciano, Ryan Wood, Jake McBride, and Sean Franklin, known respectively as War, Pestilence, Famine, and Death, had taken him under their proverbial wing and introduced him to a world he'd never known existed. It was the realm of pain and delight, power and submission, and the Four Horsemen were its lords. Despite being more than a few years their senior, Zach was their apt pupil, learning all they had to teach him.

"Yes, sir," Ryan said, living up to his nickname, the pestilential bastard. "We're almost finished with the renovation, and the pool's done."

"Are you doing the cooking?"

"Hell no! Jake is."

"Now I'm tempted." Despite Jake's nickname as Famine, he was well-known for his uncannily eldritch ability to make field rations palatable. What he did with dehydrated pork patties had long been an urban legend, still spoken of with hushed reverence.

"He went to culinary school too. His food will make you think you died and went to heaven, sir."

"Well, I suppose I could visit for a few days." Zach glanced sourly around his small Grand Rapids apartment. Aside from the largest television known to man, there wasn't anything of note to keep him planted on his couch. "You got good scotch to go with my supper?"

"Only the best, sir."

Zach rolled his eyes and stopped himself from telling

Ryan not to call him sir again. It would only make things worse. "Is the play space open for business?"

"Not yet, sir. Actually..." Zach heard a power saw firing up, then a door shut, blocking the noise. "That's the one of the reasons I'm calling. Sean remembered you liked to do woodwork, and we could use your expertise for the fixtures. We've got a contractor in, but I'd rather not have an outsider work in the dungeon."

"Ah, I see how it is. You lure me in with Jake's cooking, then expect me to work?"

"We also have a thirty-year-old bottle of Glenfiddich with your name on it, sir, and you're welcome to bring a date if you're seeing anyone."

"Bribery. Sheer bribery." Zach laughed despite himself. He'd never married, and hadn't felt like playing in a long time. The one club close to him was full of youngsters who didn't know their ass from a hole in the ground.

Then again, dominance was less about age, and more about the willingness to listen and learn. Zach himself was a prime example.

It was a pity, really. Now that he was retired, he could explore a permanent relationship with someone. He'd seen too many broken relationships, and sadly, too many widows to risk it before, yet wondered now if he was too old for dating.

He'd met a few women who had been interested, but the relationships had fizzled when they realized they had nothing in common with him. A relationship, at least one with the kind of connection he wanted, didn't seem possible, and he wasn't interested in anonymous play partners.

"No, really. I wrote it myself in permanent marker. It says, Property of Daddy."

"Asshole. You aren't cute enough, or female enough to call me Daddy."

"Hell, sir. Even Sean knew whose bottle it is, and he likes those sweet littles as much as you do."

"So, no subs waiting for a Daddy, *and* I have to work?"

"You also get to be one of the first people to stay in one of our new suites. It has a view of... well, eventually it will be a restored desert garden with walking trails. The pool even has a Jacuzzi."

"Put a bratty sub in that room and I'll be there yesterday."

"Oh, we do have a brat," Ryan muttered. "There's a reason the landscaping isn't finished. I'd turn her over my knee myself except the parts she's completed are spectacular."

"Oh?"

"Yeah. That's the other reason we want you to visit. Jolene Miller doesn't give a good goddamn about any of us. All she wants is to restore the desert, and every time we try to fire her, she comes back like a bad penny."

"Sounds like a noble goal. Why would you try to fire her if she's doing good work?"

"She's demanding we move the parking lot to a space almost a mile away because it's blocking natural game trails. I'm done fucking with her, Zach. The woman needs a come to Jesus from someone she might actually listen to."

"Is she a redhead?" Zach asked, chuckling to himself. Ryan was probably too young to get the reference to the old Dolly Parton song.

"How did you know? Never mind. Will you come, sir? We could use your expertise. Our grand opening is in less than three weeks, and we're already booked solid."

"Bit off more than you can chew with her?"

Ryan muttered something uncomplimentary that would have gotten him court-martialed had they still been in the Navy. "She's a pain in my ass and should count herself lucky she's not my sub."

"Does she know she's working for a BDSM resort?"

"Yes, we told her that when we hired her."

"I see. Is she submissive? More importantly, does she have a partner?"

"She told us she's a widow, but we didn't ask if she had a partner. It's not our business, but I don't think she does." Ryan paused and Zach heard the sound of fingertips drumming on wood. "I suspect she might have been a sub though. She said a few things about our equipment list that make me think she's been in the lifestyle."

"Do you know her age?"

"I'd say early forties if I had to guess. Maybe a few years older than Sean."

Jolene sounded fascinating, but Zach had no intention of butting in where he wasn't wanted. "I see. And what do you expect me to do with her?"

"Sir, we might have gotten you started with kink, but you do the same magic with bratty subs that Jake does with food. You're literally the only person we could think of who Jolene might listen to, and it has to be done before she makes good on her threat to go to the press saying we're killing innocent desert creatures."

"Are you?"

"Of course not! I want the entire property restored to what it was a hundred years ago, and that includes the wildlife. I'd love to help her, but we can't give her everything she wants without going out of business before we even open."

This was an opportunity Zach couldn't pass up. He'd never been able to resist a brat, and the more he heard about Jolene Miller, the more he wanted to meet her. She sounded like the perfect challenge to bring him out of his bored funk, and he looked forward to meeting a woman close to his own age.

"I'll send you my flight information after I make my reservation. With luck, I can be there in time for supper."

———

JOLENE

Humming softly, Jolene dug a small hole some yards away from the paved hiking trail. Although she wasn't a fan of concrete in a natural environment, it was necessary to make the trail accessible to guests with mobility challenges and keep everyone else from putting their big clomping feet on her plants. It had been her suggestion in the first place, and one of the few that hadn't turned into an argument with her employers, the bastards.

Jolene had grown up not thirty miles from The Majestic, now known as Club Apocalypse, and her first job had been waiting tables in the diner where the restaurant now stood. She and her late husband Ben had met there, and had even held their wedding reception in the pool area. The downward spiral for the vintage Route 66 motel had already begun before she and Ben started dating, but it had brought them together.

Ben would have been tickled to know what the new owners were doing with the place. Letting out a sigh, she tried not to think about it. He'd been gone almost five years, but she was sure he'd have talked her into purchasing a membership.

Maybe it was dumb, but she wanted to restore The Majestic for Ben. If she made it look like it used to, she could keep hold of that small piece of him.

The Horsemen had promised her free rein to clean up the

damage left by thirty years of neglect and outright malefi-cence. The old trailer where a meth lab blew up was the first thing to go, as was the makeshift junkyard of motorcycle parts and trash. It was far harder to repair the years' worth of ATV and dirt bike trails that had undermined the scant topsoil into a dust bowl. Unfortunately, her free rein came with enough strings to suspend even her wide ass in a Shibari tie.

She heard soft footsteps behind her and huffed out an irritable sigh. "I'm busy, Pest. You can try to fire me again later."

The footsteps stopped, and she heard an unfamiliar male chuckle that made something she hadn't felt in years twinge deep in her core.

"You aren't the first one to call him Pest."

Instead of looking up, she focused on easing the fragile endangered cactus from its nursery pot. As much as she wanted to see who had spoken, she couldn't afford a moment's inattention until she had the plant safely settled in its new home.

"I imagine that's true. Who are you and why are you here?"

"I'm here to help you."

"I thought the boys didn't have the funds to hire another landscaper." Holding the delicate cactus in a gloved hand, she carefully tapped the dirt surrounding the shallow root ball, then surrounded it with stones to keep it in place.

"They're not boys," he corrected. "And I'm not a landscaper."

"I have jeans older than they are." Knees creaking, Jolene stood and brushed the dirt off her coveralls, then turned to face the stranger.

Well. Hello, Daddy.

With the heavy muscularity of a real man who took care of himself, he was a touch under six feet, making it comfortable to meet his dark blue eyes surrounded by laugh lines. His gray hair was cropped short, revealing a wide forehead over a straight Roman nose. A grizzled beard couldn't quite hide the dimple in his chin.

"Zach Stratton," he said, holding out a hand.

Quickly swallowing a mouthful of drool, she got her mind off the bulge in the front of his jeans and grasped his hand firmly. She might be a middle-aged widow, but she wasn't blind and could appreciate a fine-looking man as much as the next person.

"Jolene Miller. It's a pleasure to meet you. If you'll follow me, I'll show you where I need help."

"Sir."

She stopped walking and turned to face him, hands on her hips. "Excuse me?"

"You can call me sir, although I prefer Daddy."

The bark of laughter came without warning. "Sure thing, Daddy. At least you're old enough to claim it without looking like an idiot. If you're finished with the introductions, I need you to grab a shovel and help me dig the resinbushes out from the trailhead."

"How long have you been out here?" he asked, hands still in his pockets.

"I got here at dawn. Why?"

"And water? Have you had anything to drink?"

"I'd be dead of heatstroke otherwise. Are you here to help or ask dumbass questions?"

"Well, that means you've been working around ten hours. I'm thinking it's time for baby girls to have their supper."

Jolene stared at him for several seconds, then shook her head. "Did Pest call you to force me to leave?"

He grinned, deepening the lines around his mouth. It was a good smile, warm and engaging, and she caught what might have been interested approval in his eyes as he took a step closer to brush a piece of hair off her face.

"What makes you think that?"

Despite the heat of the day, she shivered. It had been a long time since a man had touched her, and she couldn't decide if she wanted him to stop or keep going. "Let's see, you show up out of the blue, demand I call you sir, then tell me it's time to have supper. I'm thinking the boys hired you to force me to quit."

"Well, they did." He held up a hand when she opened her mouth to speak. "But I'm not going to do that."

"That makes no sense." Sweat trickled down her back,

the hot desert air drying it almost as quickly as it appeared. "You know what? I don't have time for it. I have five hours of work to finish in an hour of daylight."

"I'm here to make a deal with you," he replied, moving to block her way. "You can either listen, or the Horsemen are going to call the sheriff to have you arrested for trespassing. Your choice, little girl."

2

ZACH

"If they so much as try it, I'll be on every news station in Arizona telling everyone about how they're destroying the desert to build their resort."

"Except they aren't." He waved a hand to indicate the truly astonishing amount of work she'd already accomplished. Compared to the surrounding terrain, the property around Apocalypse was almost ethereal with no invasive plants he could see. Zach wasn't much of a gardener, but even he could tell the difference between scrubby underbrush and the carefully tended plants set in artistic groupings some distance from the concrete path.

"But they—"

"Refused to allow you to make changes that would have

a detrimental effect on their business? If they can't open and can't make a profit, how long do you think your hard work will remain intact?"

Judging by the mulish expression on her beautiful face, Jolene knew he was telling the truth. Even covered in dust and dried sweat, she was about the prettiest thing he'd ever seen. Although she had a few faint lines around her brown eyes and the corners of her generous mouth, her skin was flawless aside from a charming scatter of freckles on the bridge of her nose. Red hair, lightly sprinkled with silver, stuck out from under a wide-brimmed hat, making him want to see how long it was.

"Fine." She took off her gloves and stuffed them in her pocket. "Let me grab my water cooler, and I'll meet you in the restaurant in half an hour."

He followed her to a small lean-to containing a makeshift potting shed. Rows of plants, their pots labeled with white tape, stood on shelves, and there was a five-gallon orange water jug with a spigot sitting on an upside-down plastic crate. "I'll get that," he said, stopping her before she could reach it.

She huffed out a breath, then rolled her eyes. "Whatever. I'm pretty sure I can carry an empty water jug."

That eye roll was like a red flag to a bull. Grabbing the back of her neck, he spun her around and bent her over the table, dislodging her hat. His hand fell to her beautifully round ass in a sharp, stinging slap.

"The attitude is unnecessary, Jolene." He calmly peppered her ass with more spanks. "Daddy doesn't like when pretty little girls talk back."

Obviously experienced enough to make a spanking hurt less, her body tightened into rigidity, making him wish he had a handy ginger root plug for her bottom. It might have also helped if she hadn't been wearing those sturdy coveralls. Gritting his teeth, he delivered a harder spank to her tender sit spot, finally making her cry out and kick her booted feet.

"God dammit! Stop!"

His hand fell to the exact same spot several times. "You can stop this any time, baby. All you have to do is tell Daddy you're sorry for being a brat." Palm smarting almost as much as her ass probably was, he spanked her curved thighs. He'd have to come up with a paddle for next time.

"Bite me," she muttered, once more attempting to wriggle free.

"Don't mind if I do." Holding her still, he leaned over and sank his teeth into the pale skin under her ear, careful not to break the skin or bruise her. Much.

He licked her, tasting the salt of her sweat. She might have been working her ass off all day, but she smelled amazing and he inhaled her spicy floral perfume greedily.

Jolene gasped sharply, then stilled and let out a tiny whimper. "I'm sorry I was a brat, Daddy."

"That's my good girl." Although he had to lean close to

hear her, she'd said the right words. He kissed her neck gently to ease the sting of his bite. "Will you behave if I let you go?"

"Yes, Daddy."

He allowed himself a few seconds to enjoy her capitulation, then helped her stand, unsurprised when she jerked away and snatched up her hat and the water jug. Without a word, she spun and took off down the concrete path toward the resort.

Zach chuckled softly, enjoying the sway of her hips, then caught up and took the jug from her. Keeping her warm, callused hand in his, he said, "Hold Daddy's hand, sweetheart."

Flushing, she looked down and tried to tug her hand free. "That isn't my kink. I'm a little old for it."

"There's no such thing as being too old for a daddy. Besides, if that were true, you wouldn't be blushing."

JOLENE

Cursing her Irish heritage, she tried to ease her fingers from his grasp. "I am not blushing!"

Ben would have blistered her butt if she'd dared roll her eyes at him. However, Zach wasn't Ben, and there was no way she'd call him Daddy again. It was appalling that she'd done it in the first place, but she blamed it on the utter shock of being spanked for the first time in years.

She wasn't about to think about the stinging heat moving into her core, or how good it felt.

"You must be sunburned then. It's definitely past time to go inside." Instead of letting her go, Zach winked, then brought her hand to his lips and kissed it.

"I'm a grown woman, Mr. Stratton. You can't just automatically assume I'm a Little. Besides, I never consented to you spanking me."

He let her go long enough to open the service entrance to the kitchen, but caught her hand before she could escape. "There's nothing wrong with being Little, and I never said you were. However, I should have waited to spank you until after we'd discussed consequences for your behavior. We'll talk about it over dinner."

Although the décor had been changed, the restaurant was still the same open-plan diner it had been when she worked there as a teenager. Jake had told her it would eventually be expanded into a more formal space with a real dining room, yet she almost hated to see it go. There were so many fond memories, but she understood the necessity.

"There's nothing to discuss. I'm going to grab a sandwich and go to my suite. Enjoy your evening." She tried once more to pull her hand away. Although he wasn't hurting her, she couldn't get free of him.

He set her water jug next to the sink. "I'm glad to hear

you won't be driving home. You must be exhausted after working all day. I'll walk you back to your suite after supper."

Unscrewing the lid, he dumped the last few cups of water into the sink, then rinsed it out.

Taking advantage of the sudden freedom, Jolene made a dash for the exit. Although she'd taken one of the suites to make sure the boys didn't try to lock her out before she was finished with the garden, she wasn't about to stay a moment longer. She turned back for a split second to make sure Zach wasn't chasing her, then slammed into Jake's hard chest.

"Sorry, Jolene. I didn't see you. Are you okay?" Jake asked, taking a step back.

Of all the Horsemen, Jake McBride was the most tolerable, although she'd never understand how such an amazing cook ended up with a nickname like Famine. He was generous and easygoing, and didn't irritate her like Ryan did. Sean and Mark just made her nervous.

"I'm fine, thanks. Sorry about that." She tried to step around him, scowling when Zach blocked her path to safety.

"Good to see you again, Famine." He held out a hand, then pulled Jake into a one-armed hug. "Pest promised me you'd be cooking."

"It's good to see you too, sir." Jake went to the commercial refrigerator and pulled out a large package wrapped in white butcher paper. "I thought you and Jolene might enjoy ribeyes tonight. I also have lobster macaroni and cheese in the oven, plus fresh asparagus and a garden salad."

Jolene blinked at Jake's address, wondering why he'd called Zach sir, then decided she didn't care. She stepped out of the way before Zach could catch her again. "I'm not very hungry. Can I just get a sandwich to take back to my room?"

"As if I'd let you miss my limoncello pound cake." Jake fired up the grill, then set the steaks aside and grabbed spice jars from the overhead rack. "Didn't you say it was like an orgasm for your mouth?"

"Yes, it was delicious, but as I said—"

"An orgasm for your mouth?" Zach asked, wrapping a thick arm around her waist. "We'll definitely be having that. Jake, can we get our meals delivered to Jolene's suite in about half an hour? She and I are going to discuss her work."

"Absolutely not." She elbowed Zach in the stomach and took several steps back. "I have no idea who you are, and I'm not about to allow some strange man into my room."

"You can trust him, Jolene. Zach was our commanding officer when we were in the Navy. I can personally vouch for him."

"He's already spanked me once and didn't have permission for it, Jake. Not interested."

"You probably had it coming. Lord knows we've all wanted to spank you a time or three."

Sputtering, she glared at him, trying to ignore the twinge of hurt. "*Et tu*, Jake? I thought you liked me."

He approached her and took her hands, squeezing gently. "I do. You're sweet and funny, you've done amazing work out there, and we all love seeing the property come back to life. Unfortunately, you're demanding things we can't give you, and you won't bend. Zach is here to make you listen and meet us in the middle."

Her belly tightened and she closed her eyes against welling tears. She couldn't give up now. Leaving would mean letting go of the last piece of Ben.

"What happens if I don't?"

Sobering, Jake sighed and turned back to his grill. "You've restored too much to complain we're destroying the environment, so going to the press won't work as a threat anymore. We're going to terminate your employment, and you'll be charged with trespassing if you try to come back."

3

ZACH

Jolene turned and stormed away, but not before Zach caught the glint of tears in eyes which were the same color as perfectly-aged whiskey. For a brief moment, he considered following her to get some answers. Instead, he decided to give her time to cool down.

If she'd been his, he wouldn't have allowed her tantrum to go unpunished. Unfortunately, she wasn't. That didn't mean he wouldn't at least try to make things right between her and the Horsemen. It was more than clear Jolene cared as much as the Horsemen did about the old motel, but he suspected they had widely different motivations.

"Which suite is hers?" he asked after a moment's thought.

"Why?"

"Because I asked for it, and because I'm going to be delivering her supper."

"Sir, I—"

"Famine, are you disobeying a direct order?" Zach winked, letting his old friend know he hadn't been entirely serious. "Have it ready in forty-five minutes. I need to talk to Pest."

Jake rolled his eyes and threw his hands in the air. "East wing, room 120 at the end of the hall on the right. Ryan is in his office, just past the laundry room."

"Actually, hold dinner for a bit. I want to talk to all four of you."

There was something Zach was missing. Jolene's unexpected reaction had been too strong for such a self-assured woman and he needed more information before confronting her. Still thinking, he followed Jake down the corridor to a surprisingly large office containing a battered conference table and four chairs.

"Captain Stratton, it's good to see you," Sean Franklin said, holding out his hand.

"You as well, Death." Zach returned the handshake, then turned to Mark Luciano. "Still being a cantankerous fucker, War?"

Mark grunted, then cracked a wry smile. "You haven't changed a bit, Grim, but I'm surprised you don't have a sweet little girl on your arm."

Leave it to War to remember his old nickname. "You know me, I prefer the spicy ones." Zach propped a hip against the table, facing the other men. "Tell me what you know about Jolene. What's her history?"

"She grew up in Holbrook. That's about half an hour east of us," Sean said.

"We also know she's been working as a landscape architect specializing in arid environments. She's been a consultant with the Arizona Department of Natural Resources for about fifteen years," Ryan added.

"Any personal details?"

"Just that she's widowed. She didn't mention any children, but we didn't pry into her private life."

"Hmm." Crossing his hands behind his back, Zach paced around the room. "Do you know if she had any connection with the motel when it was open before?"

"It's possible. She's the right age to have worked here as a teenager." Ryan scratched the stubble on his jaw and stared out the window for a moment. "Now that I think about it, maybe she did. When she arrived, I asked her if she needed a tour to find her suite, and she said she knew the way."

Jake nodded, laughing softly. "She managed to get the old jukebox working in the diner. She mentioned there was a trick to it."

"I think we can safely assume she has some personal

connection to The Majestic," Mark said, leaning against the window sill. "The question is, what do we do about it?"

"Have you shown her the budget and renovation plans?" Zach asked.

Ryan shook his head. "No. We just gave her a number and let her go, then she started adding stuff."

Zach tried to control his irritation. Jolene might have gone overboard on her demands, but the Horsemen should have already provided the information. He didn't believe she was an unreasonable woman, and was sure she'd understand and accept the boundaries if she knew about them.

"Let me ask you something," he said, directing his words to all four men. "Do you want to fire her?"

Sighing, Ryan rubbed his face, then shared a glance with his friends. "No. She's doing a beautiful job, and was a pleasure to work with until she went off the rails."

"Do you mind if she sees your budget? It might help her understand your limitations if she can see them."

"I'm okay with it, as long as everyone else is," Mark replied. "I mean, the bank has already seen it."

Sean nodded his agreement. "It's not as if the information is classified."

"Hell, I don't even understand half of it. If she can, she's a better woman than I am," Jake added.

Ryan laughed, then handed Zach a thick, spiral-bound book. "This is our five-year plan, along with the budget.

We're willing to work with her, but a lot of it is already scheduled."

"Thank you, gentlemen." Zach tucked the book under one arm. "Jake, dinner in forty-five minutes, please. I also want the suite across from hers."

Shaking his head, Jake retied his apron. "You're still a bossy bastard. Do you want supper in her suite or yours? Also, housekeeping doesn't start until the week before we open. You'll have to take care of your own laundry."

"That's fine. I'm going to clean up and get changed, then Jolene and I are going to have a little chat. We'll have supper in her room."

He went outside and grabbed his suitcase from his rental car, then met Ryan at the front desk for his key card and a pile of fresh sheets and towels. His footsteps were silent on the thick carpet as he walked past a line of modern locks on newly refurbished doors. Muted lighting illuminated the corridor and the smell of fresh paint permeated the air. It was clear the Four Horsemen had worked their asses off to get the place cleaned up.

When he reached his suite, he swiped his card through the lock, then pushed the door open, purposely ignoring the one on the other side of the hall, behind which was his pretty little redhead.

"Boys, you've outdone yourselves." Nodding in approval, he entered the well-appointed suite, noting the sturdy furnishings and discreet tie-down points suitable for bondage. Even the luggage rack next to the closet was heavy enough to use as a spanking bench. Painted a muted gray with dark blue carpet, it was tasteful and elegant. The bathroom contained a double sink and a glass-enclosed shower big enough for three.

He made the bed, then stripped down and showered quickly, mindful of the printed warning on the back of the door. Water was at a premium in the desert, but he was used to fast showers. Unfortunately, his cock had other ideas that focused on the delectable lady across the hall. Gritting his teeth, he dried off, trying not to think about bending her over the ottoman with her ass in the air ready for a spanking.

Once he was dressed, he checked the time, then decided to go for a short walk around the property. He'd caught a glimpse of it, but he wanted to see the awning erected over the pool. It looked like it had channels to catch dew and rainfall, and he wanted to see for himself how the conservation system worked.

Zach made sure he had his key card, then left the room, frowning when he saw Jolene's door cracked open. She'd propped a white tennis shoe next to the doorjamb to keep it from closing.

Swearing under his breath, he knocked, meaning to paddle her butt for being so careless. The only people here were the Horsemen and himself, but she shouldn't have left her door open like that. When he got no answer, he considered going in to check on her, but didn't want to invade her privacy unless he was sure something was wrong.

A soft slapping sound caught his attention and he turned, relieved to see her carrying an armload of clean towels. She was wearing flip flops, shorts, and a tank top, revealing luscious, full curves. Damp hair trailed across her shoulders, curling slightly at the ends.

Scowling, she stopped a few feet away from him. "Why are you lurking in front of my room?"

"You left your door propped open. I wanted to make sure you were okay."

"As you can see, I'm fine. If you'll excuse me..." She glanced meaningfully at the door, then arched a brow.

"Here, let me help you." He reached for the stack of linens, but she stepped out of reach.

"Just hold the door for me, please. It's late, and I have an early start tomorrow."

Inclining his head, he pushed the door open, then held it for her. "Actually, you don't. We need to talk."

———

JOLENE

She absolutely hated when people said those words. Every awful event in her life had been prefaced by *we need to talk*—

her mother's death, Ben's deployment to Afghanistan not six months after their wedding.

His cancer diagnosis, and the news that it would eventually kill him.

Swallowing the choking sob threatening to explode, she dropped the stack of fresh towels on the bed and wondered if she'd be able to hold it together long enough to get Zach Stratton out of her room. She took a deep breath, held it for five seconds, then let it out, hoping it would be enough.

"Can... can it wait until tomorrow? I'm too tired to deal with you." She grimaced at the catch in her voice, yet there was nothing for it but to bully her way out of the situation.

"I'm actually hoping our chat will help you get along with the Horsemen. I—" A knock on her door interrupted him. Scowling, he opened it, then allowed Jake to push a room service cart into the room.

"As promised, ribeyes with all the trimmings," Jake announced. "Medium rare for Jolene, and still mooing for the Captain." Folding an arm across his trim abdomen, he bowed. "Supper is served."

"Don't let her lock me out," Zach replied, striding out the door. "I forgot something."

The delicious smells emanating from the cart nearly knocked her out of her melancholy, but she still didn't want to talk to Zach. Or anyone else, for that matter. Before she could think of a way to get Jake out of her room, Zach returned, carrying a black spiral-bound book. Giving Jake a pointed look, he jerked his head toward the door.

"Well, I'll be going." Jake edged past Zach into the corridor. "Just leave the cart—"

Zach shut the door in his face, cutting off his words. Turning to her, he dropped the book on the dresser and crossed his arms over his chest. "Care to tell me why you're just about to cry, Jolene? Did Jake say something I need to kick his ass for?"

God damned daddy doms. Although she didn't want to compare him to Ben, they had the same deep, authoritative tone that turned her knees to rubber and made her want to spill all her secrets. Was it some woo-woo magic shit or what?

She turned away and squeezed her eyes shut, praying he'd give her enough time to pull herself together. "No. I'm fine, but as I said, I'm very tired. I'd like you to go, and take the food with you."

She heard him moving behind her and hid a sigh of relief, thanking her lucky stars he'd finally gotten the hint.

"You were a beautiful bride," he said suddenly. "This was taken out by the pool, wasn't it?"

Jolene spun and her belly flipped as he picked up her wedding photo. "Don't touch that!"

She darted across the room and jerked it from his hands, inadvertently dropping it. With a sharp snap, the frame caught the edge of the dresser and fell to the carpet. Ben stared up at her, his brilliant grin hidden by a crack in the glass. Her knees buckled and she fell, then cradled the photo in shaking hands.

"Get out," she whispered softly, trying to hold back tears. This entire trip had been a waste of time. Restoring The Majestic wasn't going to bring Ben back, and every time she passed by the diner where they'd spent so much of their youth made it that much harder to let him go.

Without warning, Zach knelt in front of her, his warm, callused palms sliding over her shoulders. The scent of his aftershave washed over her in a teasing cloud of evergreen and citrus. Refusing to look at him, she held her breath against it, unwilling to admit how good he smelled.

"I'm sorry, sweetheart." He hugged her, his soft voice wrapping around her as tightly as his arms. "I didn't mean for that to happen. Are you okay?"

"Please, just leave." Jolene hated how weak she sounded, but if Zach stayed one single second longer, she was going to lose her shit and melt down in front of him. Goosebumps prickled on her arms and she drew in a shuddering breath as he let her go and eased the broken frame from her suddenly nerveless fingers.

Cursing softly, he turned her hand over. "Let's get you into the bathroom, baby girl. You cut the crap out of your hand."

To her surprise, blood dripped from a deep cut on her palm. She didn't have a chance to protest before he helped her stand, then picked her up and carried her into the bathroom.

Fucking perfect.

Biting down hard on her lower lip, she squeezed her eyes shut. "I'm fine. Please leave."

"Shh." He set her down and gently held her hand under cold running water, then hummed softly as he washed the cut and wrapped it in a clean hand towel. Wrapping an arm around her, he led her from the bathroom, then sat on the couch and pulled her into his lap. "We won't talk about anything, baby, I promise. Just let me hold you for a while."

Jolene counted herself a strong woman. She'd been a rock for her two children when their father died. Taking care of his estate was a snap. She hadn't even cried at his funeral. Well, not much anyway. But the tears came now, at the worst possible time, and she couldn't stop them.

Maybe this once she could let someone take care of her. Just for tonight.

4

ZACH

Rocking Jolene in his arms, Zach mentally recited all the English curse words he knew, then started on German, French and Spanish. He was halfway through Russian before Jolene's sobs tapered off and she fell asleep. Carefully, he checked her hand, making sure the bleeding had stopped. The cut wasn't bad enough to need stitches, but Jolene wouldn't be working for a while.

He sent a quick text to Ryan, asking him to bring a first aid kit, but to let himself in quietly. He'd been their field medic back in the day, and Zach was sure he still had the skills and supplies necessary to deal with Jolene's injury. Using his handkerchief, he carefully wiped the tearstains away, then settled her more securely in his lap.

Knowing why she'd been so determined to restore the motel's landscaping didn't make him feel any better, especially since it wouldn't solve the immediate problem with the Horsemen's budgetary constraints. Hell, he didn't know if there was a workable solution. He hadn't had time to look at the documents they'd given him.

He also had no idea why she'd melted down so quickly and without warning. It hadn't been just the damage to her wedding photo. She'd been upset before it was broken. He'd need to get to the bottom of that before he could try to make things right between her and the Horsemen.

This was why he'd never married. Zach couldn't stand the thought of leaving a woman behind, and most of his military service had been spent in war zones. He allowed himself a quiet moment to curse the man in the photograph for leaving her, even though it was ridiculous. People usually didn't die on purpose.

It was also ridiculous to be jealous of a dead man.

"Poor baby girl," he whispered softly, inhaling her floral perfume. "I'm so sorry."

The lock clicked and Ryan eased himself in the room, blinking in surprise at seeing Zach with Jolene asleep in his arms. Zach held a finger to his lips, then beckoned him closer.

"Grab that picture off the floor and fix it before she wakes up," he said, hoping the hoarse whisper wouldn't wake her. "Get rid of the food too. I'll make her something if she's hungry later."

Nodding, Ryan crouched to retrieve the broken frame, then let out a softly hissed curse as he stared at the photograph. "I'll take care of it. Why did you need the first aid kit?"

Gently and ever so slowly, he eased Jolene's clenched fist from under her chin. "She cut herself on the glass. I already cleaned it and got the bleeding stopped. She just needs a few butterfly closures and a wrap."

His touch surprisingly delicate for a man with hands the size of dinner plates, Ryan took care of the cut quickly and without waking her. "Don't let her pick up a shovel tomorrow."

"No intention of it." Zach gave the king-sized four-poster bed a considering glance. "Do you think we can get her into bed without waking her?"

Ryan leaned down, then laid a finger against the pulse under her ear. "Probably. She's out. Three weeks of fourteen-hour days must have finally caught up with her."

He grunted in response, unwilling to chew on Ryan for letting her work like that. Jolene wasn't Ryan's sub, and judging by what he'd seen and heard, she'd have ignored him and done as she pleased anyway.

Although Zach wanted to say he was still man enough to stand with Jolene in his arms without waking her, his back and knees would object. "Take her for a second so I can get up."

"Yes, sir." Ryan slid his arms under Jolene's body, then slowly lifted her from Zach's lap. Sighing, he shook his head. "Poor baby girl. It's no wonder she busted our balls. I feel like shit now."

"You didn't know." Zach rose and turned down the sheets, allowing Ryan to lay her on the bed. "Thanks."

"No problem." Ryan brushed a piece of hair off her face. "Do you want me to sit with her?"

Zach tried not to bite his friend's head off for the suggestion. Like all the Horsemen, Ryan was a decent man with a strong sense of duty. The question didn't surprise him, but he wanted to take care of Jolene himself.

"I'll do it."

"Okay. I'll have Jake wrap your supper if you want it later."

Once Ryan pushed the cart from the room, Zach used a towel to block the door and crossed the hall to his suite. After changing into a T-shirt and sleep pants, he returned to Jolene.

As he was considering the somewhat dubious comfort of the couch, Jolene whimpered softly and brought her knees to her chest, but didn't wake up.

He slid into bed with her, then settled down and spooned her against his chest, his arms wrapped tightly around her. She quieted almost immediately with a soft sigh that made his heart clench. Although she'd probably be pissed in the morning, he wanted her to have decent rest. It was clear she hadn't been getting it.

Closing his eyes, he allowed himself a smile of satisfaction. Despite the less than ideal circumstances, he did indeed have his bratty sub. Zach didn't know if things would work out between them, but Jolene was the first woman to catch his interest in a very long time.

All he had to do was make things right between her and the Horsemen, help her with her grief, and convince her to take a chance on a beat-up old veteran.

It was a campaign he didn't intend to lose.

———

JOLENE

Something woke her and Jolene's eyes snapped open, then slammed shut just as quickly at the glaring sunlight shooting into the room through a gap in the drapes. She didn't know how she'd managed to sleep past dawn, nor did she understand why she was fully dressed and buried in so much bedding it felt like she was smothered.

She wriggled, but the sheets tightened around her, making her sleep-muddled brain come online. Gasping, she inhaled the scent of evergreen and citrus mixed with warm male musk. Jolene controlled the atavistic urge to strike out to protect herself. Zach wasn't going to hurt her, and he was covered in sleep pants and a shirt. She might not want him around, but her instincts told her that much. Nothing could explain why being in his arms felt so good, and she refused to acknowledge it.

"Settle down, baby girl. It's not time to wake up yet."

"Why are you in my bed, Captain Stratton?"

"Zach, or Daddy, please. I'm retired." He tugged her close and buried his face in her hair. "Go back to sleep."

"Whatever." She tried to roll away, huffing irritably when he wouldn't let her go. "I have to get to work."

"No. Not until your hand heals."

"I'm fine. I'll just wear gloves." To be fair, her hand was a little sore, but all she planned to do was plant the last few prickly pears left in the potting shed and be on her way. She'd already worn out her welcome, and nothing she did would matter in the grand scheme of things. If she kept moving, she could be on the road by midafternoon and back in Flagstaff before supper.

"I said no. We'll get up in a few hours, have a nice brunch, then—"

Jerking her arm loose, she drove her elbow into his gut and lunged away. Unfortunately, he caught her arm, stopping her escape. Before she could voice a protest, he had her turned over his lap.

This time, there was no heavy coverall protecting her and he didn't bother with a warmup. The sound of his hard hand against her ass was a shock to her ears, and the blossoming sting sent electrified pulses through her body.

Another flurry of spanks landed on her upturned butt, making her tighten against them. Ben would have... She cut the thought off. Ben was gone and wouldn't be shoving a piece of ginger in her ass to keep her from clenching her muscles. Aside from that, Zach spanked a lot harder than Ben ever had, and the more she tightened up, the harder he spanked.

"We don't hit, Jolene," he said calmly, delivering a sharp spank to the crease between her ass and thighs which wasn't covered by her thin shorts.

"What—" She inhaled, choking on a cry as he delivered another sharp slap to the exact same spot. "You're spanking me, asshole! What do you call that?"

Without warning, he yanked her shorts down and continued spanking her. "An attitude adjustment. And watch your language."

"I don't consent!"

He paused, then rubbed her abused ass, driving the heat from her roasted butt deeper into her core. "Do you know what a safeword is?"

"I... yes, of course."

Hers used to be *ragweed*.

"Safeword, then. Say red and everything stops."

Jolene opened her mouth, but the word wouldn't come,

no matter how hard she tried. Instead, to her absolute disgust, tears slid down her face and she choked out a sob.

The minute things hadn't gone her way, she'd become an utter bitch to her employers and to Zach. They hadn't deserved it, but the harder they resisted, the nastier she got until she couldn't stop. It was her own damned fault for ruining everything.

"That's my good girl."

Zach's soft whisper seeped into the desiccated, abandoned crevices of her heart, making her cry harder as he helped her sit on his lap and wrapped her in a hug so tight it almost stopped her breathing. Unfortunately, it did nothing to stop her chokingly wretched sobs. Humming softly, he rocked her, stroking her back with gentle hands until the crying jag eased.

Her head ached from the pressure in her sinuses, but she felt lighter, somehow, more at peace with herself and what she needed to do. This time, when she moved to get off his lap, he let her go.

Using a corner of the sheet, she wiped her face, then got out of bed. Unable to meet his eyes, she lowered her head and took a step back. "Thank you, Daddy."

Without waiting for him to answer, she spun and went into the bathroom and closed the door behind her, then undressed and got into the shower. The cold water soaked the bandage on her hand, but it eased the sting in her butt and cleared her head.

The door opened, making her jerk with surprise and turn. Zach stood, visible through the clear glass of the shower door.

His appreciative gaze made butterflies take flight in her belly. Instinctively, she sucked in her tummy, then relaxed. She was too old to pretend to be anything but what she was —a woman on the wrong side of forty with her first grandchild on the way.

"I'm not done with you yet, baby girl." Stripping off his shirt and pants, he joined her, hissing as the cold water struck his shoulders.

Although somewhat softened with age, he was heavy with muscle. His abdomen was trim with a pronounced six-pack and crisp black and silver hair decorated his chest, narrowing into a treasure trail leading to his groin. Flaccid, but swelling before her eyes, his thick cock nestled in a thatch of wiry hair.

He adjusted the tap to warm the water, then poured body wash into his hand and massaged the tension from her shoulders. "I'd have thought we were old enough not to need cold showers."

"We should turn it off until we're ready to rinse." Although true, it was a dumb thing to say. Nothing else remotely intelligent had leapt to mind. Jolene couldn't decide whether she wanted him to stop or keep going. It almost felt like she was cheating on Ben, yet Ben flat-out ordered her to find someone new after he was gone. Even the kids had been trying to set her up on blind dates, but she hadn't been interested.

Until now.

It made her wonder if Ben was looking down on her, and tired of her disobeying his final order, delivered Zach to make her behave. She chuckled inwardly at the fanciful thought, but it sounded so much like something Ben would do, she couldn't resist a smile.

"Hmm."

He shut off the tap and washed her, his soapy hands gliding over her less than pert breasts and down her pouchy belly. He spent almost no time soaping her mound, yet the glancing contact was electrifying. Her breathing stalled and she let out a gasp, thanking her lucky stars she hadn't stopped regular trips to her aesthetician for waxing.

With gentle hands on her hips, he turned her to face him, then knelt and washed her legs and feet, lifting each one carefully to massage the arches. He rose, then worked shampoo into her hair, his strong fingers on her scalp nearly sending her to the tile in a boneless heap of relaxation.

His touch was more sensual than sexual, but she couldn't ignore his rigid shaft brushing against her hip. It was both a tease and a promise, and part of her wanted to do something... naughty.

5

ZACH

He bathed quickly, using Jolene's floral body wash, then turned on the taps so they could rinse. Shower sex was good in a pinch, but not when there was a comfortable bed twenty feet away and they were supposed to conserve water. He wanted time to savor his treat. He stopped the thought in its tracks before it went any further.

It was going to kill him, but he had every intention of making himself wait until Jolene made the first move. Although he'd spanked her, held her when she cried, and even woken up next to her, they'd just met. The least he could do was give the woman a full twenty-four hours before pawing her like a teenaged boy.

"What's put that sweet smile on your face, baby girl?" he asked, wrapping a towel around her hair.

The smile faded slightly and she lowered her eyes. "I guess you could say I got a wakeup call. I also owe you and the boys an apology. I'm sorry I was such a pain."

Gently, he patted her dry, then wrapped her in a fresh towel. Helping her sit on the toilet, he replaced the bandage on her hand to give himself time to formulate what he wanted to say. Leaning close, he laid his palms on her cheeks and kissed her forehead.

"I'm so very sorry for breaking your photograph, and I understand how much this project means to you."

"You didn't break it. That would be me because I had a tantrum." Flushing, she picked at the edges of the bandage. "But I realized something this morning."

"What's that?"

Her eyes glistened, but she tried another smile. "I thought restoring the landscaping would be a way to honor my husband's memory, but I don't need it. I have two beautiful children, and in a few weeks, I'll have a grandbaby to cuddle. I think Ben would understand."

Although he wanted to ask how long it had been since her husband's passing, he decided against it. Grief didn't have a set timeline. Instead, he said, "You've done outstanding work. I'm excited to see what it will look like when you're finished."

Laughing softly, she shook her head and opened the

door. "I am finished, aside from a few hours to plant the last of the specimens in the shed. After that, I'll apologize to the boys and be on my way."

Well, that wasn't going to work for him at all. Zach had no idea what she'd originally planned, but she most definitely wasn't done. Before he could reply, she took a step from the bathroom, still squeezing the last of the water from her hair.

He looked over her shoulder and caught sight of a room service cart in the center of the room. Swearing softly, he grabbed her around the waist and spun her behind him.

She blinked in surprise and pulled back, tugging the towel over her chest. "What the—"

"Stay here. Someone brought us breakfast, and I want to make sure they left."

"Really? I hadn't even noticed." Squeezing his arm, she pecked his cheek with a kiss. "Thank you. That would have been awkward."

He didn't bother with a towel and strode into the room. If any of the Horsemen were still hanging around, they'd get to see his hairy ass. Thankfully it seemed they'd had enough sense to find something better to do. There were even fresh tracks of a vacuum cleaner, particularly around the dresser where there might have been broken glass. The sound must have been disguised by the shower.

"It's all clear, baby. You can come out, but we'd both better put on some clothes before we eat."

"Okay, Daddy."

Zach wanted to strut like a rooster. He hadn't figured on her calling him by his preferred address on her own so quickly. Hopefully that meant she'd be willing to stick around long enough to allow him to come up with a new proposal that would work for everyone.

"Oh, mercy."

She hurried to the dresser, but stopped before she reached it. Covering her mouth with her hand, she stared at her wedding photo, newly matted and reframed. The mat had cutouts of what looked like postcards from The Majestic's heyday, and it obviously delighted her. The Horsemen did good work when they put their minds to it.

"Do you like it?"

She spun and leaped into his arms, peppering his face with kisses. "It's amazing, thank you so much! How did you get a new frame so fast, and where did you find those old logo images?"

"As much as I'd like to take the credit, I asked Ryan to fix it. It was him or one of the others."

Her smile didn't fade. If anything, it got bigger. Cupping his jaw with one callused palm, she kissed him. It was a gentle, tentative kiss, as if she was learning how all over again. Maybe she was.

Keeping his hands on her hips, Zach resisted the urge to deepen their kiss and let her have her way. He wanted to call it a reward for being a good girl, and while it was, he didn't want to scare her off.

All he had to do was convince her to stay. If it took a few of the leather restraints in his play bag, so be it.

Letting out a soft giggle, she broke their kiss and blushed. "I'm sorry, I should have asked first."

"You never need permission to kiss me, sweetheart." Turning her to face the dresser, he swatted her ass gently, then grabbed his discarded sleep pants and T-shirt from the bathroom and dressed. "I'll be right back, and then we'll eat."

"Okay. My key card is..." She frowned, then went to the closet and crouched. "Sorry, right here. I forgot to take it out of my coveralls yesterday. You can let yourself back in."

He took the card, then kissed her cheek. "Be right back."

After letting himself into his suite, he dressed hurriedly in the jeans and boots he'd brought for work, plus an old T-shirt. By the time he got back, she'd already laid out their food and poured coffee into two cups.

"I thought you were going to get dressed." Frowning, he pointed at her tank top and shorts. At least she was wearing socks.

"I wear this under my coveralls and didn't want to eat in them."

"Well, you're not going to be working today anyway." He sat across from her and lifted the cloche from a massive plate of steak and eggs. Although he knew the steak was likely from the night before, it looked delicious.

"I just have to find homes for a few dozen plants." She sipped from her cup and let out a hum of pleasure. "Jake makes the best coffee."

He doctored his coffee with a splash of cream and took a sip. "Show me what to do and I'll take care of them."

Her fork scraped across the plate and she dropped it, then stared at him with wide eyes. "Really? You mean it?"

"I'm certainly not letting you pick up a shovel for at least another week." He cut into his steak and took a bite, wanting to moan in pleasure. Even rewarmed, it was about the best piece of beef he'd ever tasted. He'd even say it was almost as good as Jake's pork patty parmesan made from field rations.

Her smile dimmed and she pushed her plate away. "Zach, I'm leaving this afternoon."

"I see." He took bite of his eggs, then looked up at her. "If you're after another spanking, all you have to do is ask."

"Excuse me?" Eyes narrowed, she glared at him.

"You're not leaving. Eat your breakfast before it gets cold."

"Everything is done except pulling the resinbushes from the trail head. They can hire someone else or do it themselves."

"We're going to talk to them about that later. After breakfast, we'll compare their budget to your wish list, and see what we can do to get you and the Horsemen to meet in the middle."

———

JOLENE

Just when she thought Zach might be a pretty decent guy, he turned around and proved her wrong. It was one thing to let him handle the few plants that were left, but quite another to autocratically decide she couldn't leave.

The job was finished. Well, the parts she'd originally contracted were done. Money for the additions she'd wanted wasn't going to be found if it had already been spent on something else, and she felt like a heel for demanding it.

"Zach, I've already finished everything they wanted. I was in the wrong to ask them for more, and I will be apologizing, but I can't make them—"

He gazed at her steadily and she resisted the urge to squirm, her tender butt reminding her of the consequences. "Eat half of that steak and then we can talk about it. There's still a spanking in your future if you decide to argue."

Gritting her teeth, she cut a bite from the steak. Although Jolene usually loved Jake's food, she was too distracted to enjoy it. Surprisingly, her appetite came back after the first few bites, and she finished her breakfast under Zach's watchful eye.

"Do you want your toast?" he finally asked.

"No, thank you. I'm full."

"All right." He cleared the table, placing their dishes on the cart, then retrieved the spiral-bound book from the couch. Returning to his chair, he laid it between them. "This is the budget and five-year plan for Club Apocalypse. Are you ready to go through it with me?"

"I'm not sure how it's going to help, but okay."

The boys had already told her they didn't have the money for anything else. Letting her see their financial information wasn't going to change it, but she obediently scanned the documentation.

Against her better judgment, Jolene soon became engrossed in the detailed plans and marketing studies the Horsemen had done. There was even a yearly budget item for upkeep of the landscaping. It was all very well done, but as she'd suspected, there wasn't any slop. Every penny was accounted for.

Zach read carefully, the skin between his brows wrinkled with concentration. Leaning forward, she touched his hand.

He glanced up at her, his expression softening into a smile. "Hmm? Did you find something?"

"No. They were very thorough." She pulled the book away from him and closed it gently. "I admire them very much for what they're doing, and I think it's going to be a great success."

Scowling, he leaned back in his chair and crossed his

arms over his chest, pinning her with an icy stare. "I didn't think you'd give up so easily."

"I'm not really giving up." Rising to her feet, she retrieved her coveralls and boots from the closet, then dressed. She grabbed sunscreen from the bathroom and applied it liberally to her face before stuffing the bottle in her pocket with her phone. "I was asking for things I'd have wanted if I was developing or refurbishing a nature reserve or a state park. This is a business, and has different needs."

"So, you're telling me you don't want to move the parking lot?"

"Ideally, yes, but as I said, this is a business." Laughing softly at herself, she shook her head. "To be honest, I was an idiot. My late husband and I always used to talk about buying the old place and turning it into our own private little nature preserve getaway, and..." She sat to put her boots on and let the words trail off, unsure how to put her feelings into words.

She might be able to put on a happy face for Zach, and give the Horsemen the apology they deserved with grace, yet the taste of disappointment was bitter in her throat. It was her own damned fault though. Restoring The Majestic had been her dream, but it hadn't been fair to impose it on them when they had their own vision of what it should be.

"And?" Kneeling at her feet, he brushed her hands away and tied her boot laces.

"The boys will make better use of it than I would have. I'm happy to let them take care of it."

She tried to stand, but he laid his hands on her thighs to keep her in her seat. "It seems to me you're making a lot of excuses. Care to tell me why the sudden change of heart?"

Those damned blue eyes, so different from Ben's warm brown, seemed to drill deep into her, turning over things she'd thought long buried.

Physical desire and the need to submit. To let go with a partner and trust they'd be there to catch her. Yet she couldn't let herself become that vulnerable ever again.

"Isn't that what everyone wanted?" She tried to stand again, but he wouldn't let her up. "As long as the property owners are satisfied with the landscaping, I'm perfectly fine leaving it the way it is."

"What about the wildlife?" He stood, then offered a hand to help her. "Ryan told me you wanted the parking lot moved because it was blocking game trails. You were worried about too many animals being hit, right?"

She shrugged, wishing he'd stop talking about it. "Yes, but it would probably be cheaper to have the state drop the speed limit to make people slow down."

Grinning broadly, he wrapped an arm around her waist, then escorted her to the door. "There you go! That's exactly what I wanted when I asked you to meet them in the middle."

"Great, so glad to have helped," she muttered, grabbing her hat. "I need to finish up so I can get on the road."

Zach laughed and tapped her nose. "Nope. Unless you have another job scheduled, you're going to help me with the dungeon. Ryan says it isn't finished yet."

"Are you serious? They open in less than a month!" She turned to head toward the newly constructed addition, meaning to give the boys a piece of her mind. "What the hell have they been doing, aside from pestering me?"

His blue eyes crinkled with amusement, and she couldn't help but return his smile, despite her better judgment. She should finish her business and get on home, but there was just something about Zach that made her want to stay.

It was more than physical attraction, although there was plenty of that to go around. Maybe it was the novelty of finding a man close to her own age who was actually interested.

He held out a hand, large and as callused as hers was after a lifetime of gardening. "Do we have a deal, Jolene? I help you finish the garden, and you help me in the dungeon?" Leaning close, he added, "It needs a submissive's touch. Can you imagine how badly they'll mess it up by themselves?"

Sighing, she shook her head. "Zach, the boys don't want me around anymore. I've already overstayed my welcome as it is."

"No, you haven't." He took her hand and pulled her

outside into the bright sunlight. "You just had some crossed signals and missed communication. We got that straightened out, so it's time to get to work."

"I'm not sure how you can call being threatened with arrest a crossed signal."

"Don't worry. They're not going to do it, because I'll leave too."

He walked faster, making her jog to keep up. "Zach, wait! I—"

They rounded the utility building next to the pool and she froze. All four Horsemen stood next to her potting shed, dressed for work. There was a lounger set up under one of the pool umbrellas, along with a table and her water jug.

"It's about time you two got up!" Ryan called, grinning at them. "We've been waiting for hours."

"No, we haven't." Mark moved the water jug into the shade. "More like five minutes."

"We decided to help you." Jake strode toward her, then took her hand and led her to the lounger. "We might not be worth much for your plants, but we can all use a shovel. Your jug is already filled with the lime electrolyte solution you like."

"You wanted those bushes closest to the pool gone, right?" Sean asked, leaning on an aforementioned shovel.

Ryan helped her sit, then filled an insulated bottle for her. "And all you have to do is sit there and look pretty while you tell us what needs done."

6

ZACH

The Horsemen were doing him proud, but if they made Jolene cry, he'd take them all behind the woodshed. Her eyes were suspiciously damp as she sat gingerly on the lounger and accepted the water bottle from Ryan.

"You guys, I... I don't know what to say. You don't have to do this."

Mark shrugged and set his shovel to the base of the invasive resinbush closest to her. "We figure we can get this done in a few hours, then we'd really like to see all your ideas for the place. Maybe we can't do much right now, but we can put them in the plans for later."

Sean started digging on the other side. "I was thinking

we could have an overpass built at the property line. It would be out of the way of traffic and still let wildlife cross safely."

"The restaurant will eventually have windows looking out over the garden too. I'd like to set up an outdoor dining area and tear out some of the concrete to put in more plants." Cursing, Jake plucked a thorn from his thumb, then got back to work. "Well, in a couple of years anyway. We need to renovate the restaurant first."

"But that's not... no, it's going to cost too much," Jolene protested. "I saw your budget, and I owe all of you an apology. I shouldn't have—"

"Doesn't mean it won't be in the budget later." Ryan crouched and tugged on the woody growth. "Go wild and give us your wish list, baby girl. It doesn't all have to be done at once."

Her eyebrow arched at the diminutive. Deciding to get her moving before she started chewing on Ryan, Zach pulled her to her feet. "Let's get those plants in the ground while you think about it, sweetheart. Don't forget your water."

Shaking her head, she went to the shed and retrieved a few tiny pots from a shelf. He took them from her, then gazed at her sternly. "What part of you aren't working today wasn't clear?"

"But I—" She pursed her lips into a mutinous line and let out a huff. "Fine. Just put them in that wagon, but don't touch them with your bare hands. We have to hike about a quarter of a mile toward that ridge south of us."

"Baby girl, you're working up to a spanking, and I'm sure you don't want me to do it in front of the boys. Care to rephrase that?"

She blinked, then lowered her head. "Sorry. Will you please load the plants into the wagon, Daddy?"

Zach stroked a finger across her jaw, then leaned close to kiss her. "That's my good girl," he murmured, enjoying her blush. "Why shouldn't I touch them?"

"Several of them are prickly pear. The spines are small and hard to get out, but I have plenty of glue in case of accidents."

"Glue?"

"Yeah, you spread it over the spines, wait for it to dry, then peel it off."

Laughing softly, he loaded the wagon. "I used to do that when I was a kid."

"Me too." She reached for the wagon handle, then blushed and took a step back. "Sorry, I'm used to being by myself."

"That won't be happening anymore. Hold Daddy's hand, baby."

Giggling softly, she obeyed, but gave him a sideways glance. "You probably ought to pay more attention to where you put your feet, Daddy."

"Why is that?"

"Snakes." She bounced excitedly as they reached a stand of newly planted bushes. "I found a baby sidewinder just past those sage bushes the other day. It was cute as a button."

Instead of letting her go, he tightened his grip, unwilling to let her traipse around where she might get bitten. Zach knew he was being ridiculous though. She'd grown up here, and had to be familiar with the local wildlife.

"Will you tell me about the plants?"

"This is high desert grassland, so I'm trying to reintroduce species you'd find in Homolovi State Park. Once they're established, the forage will draw porcupines, elk, black-tailed prairie dogs, burrowing owls, mountain lions, and..." She eased her hand from his and lowered her head. "Sorry. I must be boring you silly."

"No, it's fascinating." He gestured at four large saplings arranged several feet off the trail. "Are all of those the same tree?"

"Those are Gambel oaks. I wanted to see if I could get a few shade trees going, but I'm not sure how well they'll do." She picked up the pace, striding down the trail. "Anyway, let's get the babies into their new homes."

"All right. What will we do after that?"

"I'd love to burn out that stand of *ailanthus altissima* near the dry creek bed, but it'll have to wait until the native plants are established."

"Why do you have to burn them?" Zach hadn't lied when

he said he was fascinated. Jolene obviously loved her job, and if she was willing to teach him, he was happy to listen.

"The tree-of-heaven is impossible to kill and it spreads scary fast. Think the horticultural version of Aliens." She pointed to a thickly grouped stand of trees with large leaves several yards away. "Unfortunately, birds eat the berries, and I can't try to get rid of them until there's another food source."

"You can't just cut them down?"

"Not effectively. Sprouts will grow from the stumps, and the roots produce suckers. Someone will have to mow around it to keep it from spreading. Watch out for that fire ant nest."

He sidestepped quickly, avoiding the small mound of soil. "Speaking of impossible to kill," he muttered. He'd never seen a nest in person, but he'd heard too many stories to mess with them.

"I actually have someone coming out to take care of them. He's an artist who pours molten aluminum into the nest, then digs it up when it cools and sells it. All the Horsemen have to pay is the cost of the aluminum and his gas."

"Savage."

"Satisfying," she retorted. "Have you ever been bitten by one?"

"I grew up in Michigan. The biggest pest we have is Canada geese."

"I've never been that far north." She slowed, then left the path and walked several feet away. "Here's where I want the prickly pear. Just dig some random holes about four inches deep and a foot or two apart, but keep them in a loose circle."

Under her direction, he planted the tiny cacti, carefully setting each into its new home. By the time he finished, his back and knees ached, but one glance at Jolene's blossoming smile made it all worthwhile.

"Ready to go back?" he asked, stripping off his gloves.

"Sure." She passed him her water bottle. "You need this more than I do. All I've done today is stand around."

Taking it, he drank greedily, the cold water soothing his dry throat. "I can't believe you've been doing this every day. I'm ready for a nap and some aspirin after just a few hours."

"To be fair, I can't work as fast as you do." Chuckling, she grabbed the handle of the wagon, leaving him with the water bottle. "I'm no spring chicken either. Why do you think I left those resinbushes for last?"

Neither was Zach, but he caught up and swatted her butt, then took the wagon from her. "Hush. You're perfect just the way you are."

————

JOLENE

"Will you look at that?" Zach pointed at the newly cleared area where the invasive resinbushes used to be.

"Where's a good place for a bonfire?" Ryan called, meeting them at the trailhead.

"A... what? We can't have a—"

"Seems like a perfect opportunity to get rid of those trees by the creek bed," Zach said, giving her a smug grin. "We just need some chainsaws and a couple of propane torches."

"Tempting, but no. That's a job for professional foresters. I'll move my truck around, load up the waste, and dump it in the ravine a few miles down the road."

"Spoilsport." Jake grinned at her, letting Jolene know he'd been kidding. "What's next, boss?"

"I guess pull down the lean-to. You won't need it anymore."

"Where are you going to store all your tools?" Sean leaned on his shovel, peering at her with thickly lashed dark eyes.

Jolene frowned, then stopped herself before she took a step back. Sean made her nervous, and she felt like a mouse hiding from a circling hawk under his steady gaze. "The shed behind my house, same as they've been for years."

"That doesn't work for us." Mark's footsteps were silent as he approached. They might be young, but Sean and Mark were too intense for her on a good day. Putting both of them together made her fight or flight instincts kick in.

Instead of helping her, Zach plopped his fine backside in the lounger and refilled the water bottle. Taking a drink, he held the bottle up in a toast and grinned, the big jerk.

"Sorry to hear that." Keeping her eyes on them, she walked backwards. "I'll just grab my truck and load up. You boys can take care of the rest."

Jake popped up behind her like a damned prairie dog, scaring the life from her. "We'll build Jolene a proper work-space big enough for a small tractor. She'll need it when we expand."

Flanking her to cut off her escape, Ryan said, "Behind the dungeon. It'll be out of sight, but still convenient."

"She can keep her suite." Mark moved to block her retreat. "She won't have to commute."

"That might be better." Sean slithered to her right, adding his implacable presence to the three men surrounding her. "We'll be able to keep an eye on her."

"I have to say I'm a little confused. Yesterday, you four were threatening to have me arrested, and today you want me to stay. What gives?"

Ryan took her hand and squeezed her fingers. "We figured out you weren't purposely trying to be difficult. We want you to work with us and find a way we can both have what we want."

"And if you stay, Captain Stratton will stay." Jake winked

and handed her a perfectly ripe banana with a touch of green near the stem, just the way she liked them.

"Wait! You can't—"

"We're a package deal, baby girl." Zach toasted her with his bottle, grinning like a fool.

She scowled at him, but couldn't help the warmth blossoming in her chest. The boys were trying, lord knew they were trying, and their willingness to make things right with her meant a lot. And maybe this wouldn't be a bad side hustle. She was getting close to retirement, and although she'd invested wisely and didn't need the money, Jolene didn't see herself sitting on her butt for long before she got bored.

"Also, we have restraints." Sean held up a pair of leather bondage cuffs, then took a threatening step toward her. "We'll just tie you down."

"That's not convincing me to stay," she retorted.

"Put those away, Death," Zach barked. "Well, unless she does a runner. Then you can use the cuffs."

She turned her scowl on Zach, then let out a breath. "I'll stay, but only part time, and we'll reevaluate things in six months. I'll also be keeping my house in Flagstaff, so don't think you're getting me to move in here."

"Are you sure?" Ryan asked. "We could make a suite part of your relocation."

"I'm sure. I'm expecting my first grandchild soon, and I want to be close to them."

Mark blinked, then gave her a sour glare. "No wonder you keep calling us boys. I wouldn't have guessed you'd be old enough to have grandchildren."

She arched a brow, then crossed her arms over her chest. "Thanks, I think, but I've still got a few weeks before I have to use a cane and start wearing hearing aids."

"Ignore War. He's an ass," Zach said, rising to his feet. "If we're done out here, we'll see what needs done in the dungeon."

"Let's do the resinbushes first. I'll be right back with my truck."

Shaking his head, Ryan held out his hand. "I'll get it. Give me your keys and eat your snack."

"They're in it, but I—"

Zach wrapped an arm around her waist, then returned to the lounger and sat with her in his lap. "Be a good girl and eat your banana, baby."

Jolene let out a sigh and debated telling him it was too damned hot to sit on someone's lap. Even in the shade, the temperature was approaching a hundred degrees. Taking the banana from her, he peeled it, then held it for her to take a bite. It made her feel almost childlike, but cared for in a way she hadn't felt in years. Even though she knew better, she... liked it.

One way or another, she was going to have to leave Club Apocalypse soon. Whatever might happen with Zach wouldn't last, and she couldn't afford another heartbreak. She'd just have to keep her distance until...

Her breath caught and she straightened. It would cost her this job and the chance to honor Ben's memory, but Jolene knew exactly what she needed to do.

7

ZACH

Jolene climbed off his lap the minute he loosened his grip to refill the water bottle. He hid a scowl, then passed it to her. "Where are you going?"

Instead of taking the bottle, she stepped out of reach. "It's too hot. I'm going inside."

After lord only knew how many long days under the Arizona sun, *now* she was too hot? He almost questioned her, but decided to hold his peace for the moment.

"All right." Zach got to his feet, his back still throwing a fit over all the digging he'd done. "We can watch a movie or something until it cools down, then we'll start on the dungeon."

Lowering her head, she didn't look at him. "No, I'm tired.

I think I'm going to take a nap or read for a while. I'll catch up with you later."

Frowning, he let her walk away, but wondered what was going on in her head. If Ryan hadn't gone to get her truck, he'd have almost believed she was about to attempt an escape. He wasn't sure if the Horsemen had scared her off, or if she just needed time to regroup, but he wouldn't let it stand for long.

Ryan backed a somewhat battered long-bed Dodge up to the pile of brush, then hopped out. Within moments, they had the mess cleaned up.

"Where did Jolene go?" Ryan asked, slamming the tailgate shut.

"She went inside. Said she was tired, and it was too hot." Still frowning, Zach glanced toward the motel.

"Bullshit." Jake filled a plastic tumbler from the jug and drained it. "That woman is a machine."

Mark hissed a breath through his teeth. "Think she's going to—"

Ryan jingled her keys, then stuffed them into his pocket. "No, she won't be leaving until we say so."

"Or until her grandbaby decides to come," Sean replied.

"I think she's scared." Jake folded the umbrella, tucking it under one arm.

"Of what? Us?" Ryan barked out a laugh, then climbed into her truck. "Not seeing it. I'm going to get rid of this, then grab some lunch. I'll leave the keys in the truck when I finish."

"I'll help you." Sean got into the passenger seat and they drove away.

Ignoring the aches in his back, Zach carried the lounger back to the pool, his mind working. Jolene didn't strike him as a woman who couldn't stand up for herself against the Horsemen, but something about what Jake said niggled at him. She'd been wary, yet seemed happy enough with the new arrangement until he pulled her into his lap and fed her that banana.

That meant it was him. Zach would have bet good money she'd been interested, yet her behavior said otherwise. Sighing, he tamped down his irritation and disappointment. He should have known better than to get his hopes up. She was a gorgeous, capable woman who could have had anyone she wanted—even one of the boys, despite the age gap between them. What would she want with an old man well past his prime?

When Jake set the umbrella back in its stand, Zach pulled himself together. "Show me to the dungeon, please. We'll see what needs done and I'll get started."

"Yes, sir." Jake led him into the newly constructed outbuilding and flipped a bank of light switches to illuminate a small reception area. "I know it's a little bright, but we added extra lighting for cleaning and sanitizing the equipment."

Jake drew back a curtain dividing the vestibule from the play area, revealing several boxes stacked against one wall, along with lumber. The floors were polished concrete and the unadorned walls were a smoky gray with darker sponging. Suspension rings hung from a heavy beam mounted crossways in one corner of the ceiling. He made a note to have the boys install padding under the area.

"Where's the equipment?"

Grunting sourly, Jake pointed at the boxes. "Not built yet. None of us are worth a damn with tools, and we didn't want to break anything."

"What would you have done if I hadn't agreed to come?" Despite his irritation, Zach hid a smile of amusement.

"We'd have hired someone local. That stuff is too expensive to mess with."

"Fair enough." Zach pointed at the bar. "Y'all aren't serving booze in here, are you?"

"Yes, but there's a property-wide two drink maximum if folks are playing."

"How are you enforcing that?"

"We'll have personalized drink coupons. Everybody will get two, and guests will have to show ID to make sure they don't get passed around. Folks can order more without a coupon, but they get a black hand stamp so we know not to let them scene."

"Good idea. Have you organized dungeon monitors yet?"

"For now, Ryan, Mark, Sean, and I will take turns. We'll

hire more once we get to know people." Jake grinned sheepishly, then shrugged. "Of course, you just say the word and we'll hire you on the spot."

"I'll think about it," Zach promised. He wasn't particularly attached to Grand Rapids, and having been in the Navy for most of his adult life, he didn't much care where he lived as long as he was doing something worthwhile. Maybe Jolene would change her mind and come in one day.

Deciding not to think about her, he strode to the wall of boxes and opened the closest with a penknife, recognizing the logo of a talented builder of bondage furniture on the shipping label. From the looks of it, the dark-stained wood would eventually be a very nice spanking bench.

"Where are you keeping your tools?"

"I'll get what we have." Jake jogged to the bar and pulled out a small toolbox, plus a cordless screwdriver, then returned. "Here they are."

"Thanks. What are you doing for floor covering? The subs are going to bitch if they have to crawl across this concrete. You also need padding under the suspension area."

"The mats are coming by the end of the week. We haven't thought about anything else except that polished concrete is easy to clean. Maybe floor pillows with washable covers for where they'll be kneeling?"

"Yeah." Zach started pulling pieces from the crate. "How about furniture?"

"We've got couches, tables, and chairs coming tomorrow. Art will be here before we open. We commissioned a series from Natalie Mercer in Minnesota. She and her husband are coming to oversee the installation."

He grunted in acknowledgement. Natalie was one of the most talented creators of erotic art in the world. The boys must have spent a fortune on her work.

"Aftercare space? Bathrooms? I'm assuming Ryan is going to be the standby medic."

"Through that door." Jake pointed at a red-painted steel door next to the bar. "Ten by ten cubicles with double beds. Those are already in place. Separate showers and locker rooms for men and women, plus one communal. We've got a full EMT kit set up in a triage room. We even have a portable defibrillator."

Zach blinked in surprise. The boys might have forgotten carpet, but it was clear they'd spared no expense for the important shit. "Good. I'll get these put together and the four of you can arrange everything when I'm done."

Jake shuffled his feet, then took a step backward. "Also, um, there's one more thing."

"What is it?"

"We need a cross." He pointed at the stack of lumber. "Sean thought he could build one, but... Anyway, we can't have a dungeon without a St. Andrew's cross, right?"

"Why didn't you order one with everything else?"

"The backorder was too long. It was going to be six months."

Sighing, Zach rubbed his face, then crouched to examine the wood. The heavy maple would be a bitch to cut and drill, but it was perfect for bondage furniture. "How long do I have?"

"Three weeks."

He'd have to work fast, but it was doable. "All right. Is there a hardware store nearby? I'm going to need a lot more than a cordless screwdriver."

JOLENE

After closing the door to her suite, she leaned against it and laid a hand over her heart to still its pounding. She'd hated the look of disappointed hurt on Zach's face, but it was better this way.

Or, at least that's what she kept telling herself.

Still, she'd promised to help him in the dungeon, and she knew full well the boys hadn't done shit in there. Then again, it was the perfect opportunity to up her brat game and show Zach he was better off without her.

Her course decided, she changed into fresh shorts and a tank top, then put on a full face of war paint, including a bright red lipstick that would have clashed with her hair if she hadn't had so much gray. Flip flops and a high pony tail completed the *I'm totally ready to brat your socks off* look.

Letting out a breath, Jolene gazed at herself in the bathroom mirror. She felt ridiculous, but she had to look the part. After sliding her keycard into her pocket, she strode through the empty motel to the west wing and past the diner to the end of the corridor. Instead of the glass door she was used to, it was black-painted steel to conceal what would be going on in there during operating hours.

It would be cries of pleasure and pain, the sound of leather hitting flesh, and the scent of passion. None of it would be for her though. Straightening her shoulders, she opened the door and stepped into the small vestibule, then through the curtain blocking the reception area from the rest of the club.

To her surprise, the room was empty aside from several boxes stacked against one wall. One had been opened, revealing parts that needed to be put together.

Shrugging, she extricated the pieces from the crate and grabbed the cordless screwdriver from where it had been left on the floor. It was probably against the brat code to do work without being made to, but there was no point in misbehaving if nobody was around to see it.

Besides, she really did want the Horsemen to succeed.

She found a stereo system behind the bar and turned on some music to work by, then retrieved the bag of hardware along with the assembly instructions. By the time she had the spanking bench put together, she was in a groove and assembled two more of different configurations. The bondage table gave her a bit of trouble because it was so heavy, but she managed it with only one bruised knuckle.

Knowing she'd need help with them, she left the two steel cages alone, then got to work on a wicked-looking bondage horse. Free standing with a leather bolster and tie-down points along both sides, it made her mouth dry and her pussy clench with desire as she imagined herself bound and helpless.

The music she'd chosen didn't help. What woman didn't catch the feels when Barry White started singing? Well, maybe it was John Legend these days.

Dammit.

Her fingers trembling, she inhaled the scent of leather and stroked the cushion upon which a hapless sub would rest while their dom did unspeakably delicious things to them.

"I thought you were tired and needed a nap."

Screeching in fright, Jolene jumped about ten feet in the air and tripped over the pieces of an unassembled pillory in her haste to escape. Laughing softly, Zach walked to her and held out a hand to help her up.

"Are you okay?" He ran his hands down her arms, then looked her over.

Grimacing, she rubbed her hip where she'd fallen. "You scared the shit out of me."

"I can see that." Still grinning, Zach went to one of the

benches she'd put together. "You didn't answer my question."

"What?"

"You said you were tired and needed a nap. Must have been one hell of a power nap to have all this done in less than two hours." The smile fled and he crossed his arms over his chest. "Did it also magically heal the cut on your hand?"

Shit. Jolene gathered her fraying composure and stuck her nose in the air. Bratting didn't come naturally to her, but she had to make this work. "I decided I was bored, and now I'm not. I think I'm going to go for a swim."

"Did you put the horse together first, or was it one of the spanking benches?" He picked up one of the uprights for the pillory, then scanned the floor for the bag of hardware. "I'm trying to decide which of these was your favorite."

"None of them. I have no idea what you're talking about."

"You seemed to be communing with the horse when I walked in. Maybe you liked that one the best."

Damned daddy doms. They were all too observant. She cast about for something to say that would make him give up and leave her alone. "Hardly. I was just thinking the boys bought cheap stuff. I mean, look at that crappy leather."

"Hmm." He bent and examined the fine-grained black leather. "I see what you mean. It should have been stuffed with cashmere to make it more comfortable for bratty subs, right?"

She rolled her eyes and huffed, hoping it was obnoxious enough. "Whatever. I'm out of here."

"Be a shame to mess up all that pretty makeup with a swim, baby girl."

Jolene's attempts at being a brat were obviously falling flat. Putting her hands on her hips, she scowled. "I can do whatever I want to, and you can't stop me!"

"That's true if you use a safeword," he replied mildly as he stalked her. "If you don't, you'll find you're very much mistaken."

Lord help her, she tried. All she had to do was spit out a single syllable, but it wouldn't come. His bootsteps sounded like thunder on the concrete floor, making her freeze. Her mouth dried and her tongue was thick and immobile. Every attempt she made at forcing a word—any word—past her lips met with failure.

"Tell me something, Jolene. Is it me you object to? If you're not interested, just say so." He scraped a hand through his short hair, then gazed at her with a mixture of disappointment and irritation. "I'm not a mind reader, honey, and you're blowing hot and cold worse than the old Nova I drove in high school."

She lowered her head and blinked back tears. "No, I do. I just..."

Despite herself, she wanted it. Wanted him. Needed what he had to offer. The overwhelming desire to submit and let him take care of her almost stole her breath. It wasn't safe though. Maybe he wouldn't die, but he'd leave. There were no guarantees in life, and she couldn't let herself fall again. It was too hard to pick herself back up, yet she hadn't meant to hurt him.

"Jolene, eyes."

She snapped her head up and he circled her throat with a large hand, then squeezed gently. His dark blue irises, the same color as Mormon Lake in winter, pierced her like a blade.

"Say it, little girl, and I won't tear that shirt off you and use it to tie you to the bondage horse. Red will stop my belt from hitting your ass. One single word will stop the punishment you've earned for lying, and for disobeying my order about working today."

"I..." Nothing else came out and when he loosened his hold on her throat, she licked her lips, then crossed her arms behind her back, tacitly giving him her consent.

Slowly, almost soothingly, he petted her shoulders, then leaned close to kiss her. "There's my good girl," he crooned. "I need you to say it, honey. Tell me you're okay with what's going to happen."

The door opened suddenly, making Jolene flinch with surprise.

"Hey, Captain, we—"

"Get. Out."

Zach didn't turn and kept his eyes firmly on hers, yet his soft voice carried across the room. She heard a squawk that shouldn't have come from a male body, then the door slammed before she could decide which of the Horsemen had spoken.

"Consent or walk away, baby girl."

Her throat was almost too frozen for speech, and helpless to do anything else, she nodded and managed to choke out a single word.

"Yes."

The sound of tearing fabric brought her out of her stunned stupor and she instinctively covered her chest, the tatters of her tank top falling open.

"Hands down. Don't hide yourself from me."

A muscle in Zach's jaw worked, and he pulled the shirt away from her, then tore it down the back. Holding the two pieces in his fist, he gently wrapped his free hand around her throat and led her to the bondage horse.

"Zach, I—"

"Take off your shorts unless you want those ripped off too."

His implacable expression almost had her trying to get that safeword to come out, yet she didn't want to. She was apprehensive, but not scared. At least, not yet. Swallowing hard, she tried again.

"I'm sorry, I... I didn't mean to be such a pain, and I didn't mean to insult you. Can I get a do over on today?"

"Absolutely." Zach's lips quirked into a half-smile. "After I beat your ass for lying and working when you're already hurt. You might even get a reward after your punishment if you explain to me what's going on in your head."

The smile faded and she shivered. Telling him her secrets was the last thing she wanted to do, but she was sure she could come up with something. "Yes, Daddy."

"Shorts off. Now."

Biting her lip, Jolene unbuttoned her shorts, then slid them over her hips until they fell to the floor. Without warning, he spun her around, then picked her up and set her on the horse, straddling it. She choked back a moan when the cool leather hit her damp core.

"Zach... Daddy, I think I—"

"Need to bring your knees up and lean forward on the bolster," he finished. "But how could I have forgotten your pretty blue panties?"

8

ZACH

He stretched half of her tank top and quickly tied one wrist to the polished steel ring set into the horse's wood cross member, then repeated the process with her other hand. After making sure there was a sufficient gap between her skin and the fabric, he drew a path down her spine with his closed penknife.

'Daddy, I... what are you doing?"

"Have you ever played with knives, baby?"

"No, and I don't think—"

Zach popped the blade open, cutting off her words. "Is it something that might finally drag a safeword out of you?"

Eyes wide, she tried to lift her torso off the bolster, then chewed on her lower lip. "I... no, Daddy."

Stepping behind her, he traced a delicate tiger stripe on her hip with the dull edge of the blade. He wanted to follow the path of that silvery line with his tongue and inhale the sweet perfume of her arousal into his lungs. "Tell me why you haven't used a safeword."

"I don't want to." To his surprise, she relaxed against the cushion, the tension in her spine easing as she lowered her head. Almost too softly to be heard, she added, "It won't come out because you might go away."

"Hmm." He'd have to explore that later. As flattering as it was, Zach wasn't about to do anything without the security of a safeword.

He slid the knife blade under the edge of her panties at her hip and cut them from her, then balled them up, thrilled when he felt how damp they were. Crouching, he put the wad of fabric in her hand and cupped her chin to make her look at him.

"If you can't get a word out, can you let go of those panties?" The wadded cloth fell to the floor and he leaned close to kiss her. "That's my good girl. You do that if it gets to be too much, okay? I won't go anywhere. I promise."

"Yes, Daddy."

Zach retrieved her panties, then put them back in her hand. Moving behind her, he unbuckled his belt and pulled it from the loops. The hissed sound brought goosebumps to her flesh and she shivered, making him smile. Although he wanted to draw out the anticipation, this was a punishment.

They'd hopefully have time for more entertaining possibilities later.

"Now, tell me why you're about to be punished."

"Because I lied, and because I worked when I wasn't supposed to."

"Good girl. You'll get ten, and I want you to count them. After that, it'll be over and we'll talk about what happened."

He stroked a hand over her lush ass, taking a moment to enjoy the feel of her smooth skin, then brought the belt down over the lower curve of her ass. The sound of leather hitting skin echoed in the empty space of the dungeon, and she let out a surprised shriek.

"Count, sweetheart, or I'll have to start over," he reminded her, giving her a few seconds to adjust.

"One," she gasped, wriggling slightly.

He let the belt fall again, just above the first reddening line on her bottom.

"Two!"

The number came out on a pained cry and he adjusted his third blow, making it a bit less intense. She obviously had some experience, but probably hadn't had a hard spanking in a long time—maybe not since her husband passed.

"Three."

That was better. A punishment spanking was supposed to hurt, but he didn't want to go beyond her tolerance on their first session. A dom who did that didn't get a second chance. He targeted her firm thighs for the fourth, just below her ass.

"Four! Five!" Tears thickened her voice, but she tightened her hand around the tattered panties clenched in her fist. "Six!"

By the eighth, she was sobbing uncontrollably and choked out the count, the word almost unintelligible. He considered stopping, but he'd said ten, and she still held the fabric tightly.

"Jolene, give me a color. I need to know where you are."

"G... green, Daddy." She pulled her fist to her chest as much as she was able, as if she thought he might take the safeword signal away from her.

Zach delivered the last two quickly, barely giving her enough time to count, then cut the ties holding her in place. Ignoring the twinges from his back and knees, he picked her up, then carried her through the door Jake had indicated for aftercare to the first of four small rooms.

The cubicle had a sliding pocket door for privacy, a bed with fresh sheets, a small nightstand with tissues and condoms, plus a small refrigerator with a bowl of prepackaged snacks on top. He laid her down and covered her with a blanket, then opened the fridge. To his surprise, it was already stocked with individually wrapped cheeses, fruit, and bottles of water.

As thankful as he was for it, he was going to have a talk with the boys about their priorities. Then again, maybe they'd expected him to use the play space with Jolene once the furniture was built.

"Daddy?" Jolene sniffed, then lifted her head from the pillow.

"One second, baby." He stripped off his jeans and boots, then his shirt. She'd probably want the skin-to-skin contact, although he had no intention of taking advantage of the situation.

Not yet, at least.

Using a tissue, he dried her tears, then slid in behind her. He pulled her against his chest and reached for the water. Helping her sit up, he held the bottle to her lips. "Drink, Jolene."

She sniffed and wiped her eyes with the back of her hand, then drank obediently. "I'm okay, and I... I think I'm ready to tell you everything."

"Have some chocolate first," he urged, sliding a square of candy into her mouth. "After that, we'll cuddle while we talk."

After finishing the chocolate, she laid her head on his bare chest and sighed heavily. "I've been an utter cow, and I'm sorry."

"Do you want to tell me why?" Zach tucked the blanket more tightly around them to protect her from the A/C vent above the bed. "I'm thinking it has something to do with why you melted down yesterday."

"I lost my husband, my dom, to cancer five years ago.

We both worked in the diner as teenagers and were married here. Last night..." She paused and sniffled softly. "Every time someone says 'we need to talk,' it triggers me. That's what the doctors said when we got Ben's cancer diagnosis, and when they told us he wasn't responding to treatment."

Although he'd already known of her loss, the soft whisper made his heart clench and he lowered his head to kiss her cheek. "I'm so very sorry, baby."

"Thank you." She was silent for several seconds, and all he could hear was the sound of her soft breathing. "I was okay though. I worked, finished raising my children, and... Anyway, despite my kids trying to set me up on blind dates every time I turned around, I wasn't interested until I met you."

"What happened with the Horsemen?" He wanted to know more about why she was interested in him, but she'd tell him soon enough.

She laughed softly and lifted her head, the skin around her eyes wrinkling with wry amusement. "I got it into my head to make Club Apocalypse exactly like Ben always said he wanted, and when they said no, I got stubborn."

Smirking, he tapped her nose. "You, stubborn?"

"Hush." She pushed gently on his chest, then laid her head down. "Then you came, and you're gorgeous and perfect, and it seemed like Ben was making me obey his last order to find someone else after he was gone."

"Then maybe I should thank him." Zach was hardly perfect, but decided not to argue.

"Yeah, I know, it's ridiculous." Sitting up, she wrapped the blanket around her shoulders. "I got scared. What if I get attached and you leave? Maybe not die, but what if it doesn't work? I can't do that again."

She husked out the last few words as if she was on the verge of tears. Zach wrapped his arms around her and just held her until she could compose herself. Finally, he said, "Nothing is guaranteed, honey. We get the time we get, and for a long time, I was just as afraid as you are."

"I don't understand."

"I spent most of my adult life in the Navy, and I was too afraid of leaving a widow behind to marry or even develop a long-term relationship. I missed out on the chance to have children, the grandchild you're waiting for, and..." He paused and let out a soft sigh. "Maybe something like you and Ben shared."

"I'm sorry." She turned in his arms to look at him. "Do you think it's too late for us?"

He cupped her beautiful face and lowered his head to kiss her, his tongue tracing her plump lower lip until she opened for him and deepened their kiss. She broke away and nibbled his jaw, sending electric shards of pleasure into his balls. Even with smeared makeup and black mascara streaks under her eyes, she was gorgeous.

Groaning, he pulled back, his cock urging him to take

things further. Instead of letting him go, she straddled his waist and kept kissing him.

"I don't think it's too late at all, but it's been a while for me. Maybe we should—"

Jolene rested her hands on his chest and circled her hips, rubbing herself against him. "Five years, Daddy. My virginity's grown back."

Her wet core slid over his boxer briefs, making him curse the fabric separating them. He choked on his own spit, then reminded himself he was supposed to be the dom. "I'm clean. Just had a physical, and the results are on my phone. Are you still firing live rounds, honey?"

"At my age?" She burst into laughter, then bit his nipple. "I seriously doubt it. Besides, there's condoms sitting right there."

"Naughty girl." He rolled her over, positioning her hands over her head. "Don't make me find something to tie you down again. I already cut your shirt up."

Still giggling, she wriggled under him, but didn't move her hands. "Oh, the humanity! I'm trapped by a big, bad Daddy. Whatever shall I do?"

He grinned, enjoying her sense of humor, then slid down her body, taking time to suck on her nipples and kiss her gently rounded belly. She smelled so damned good, like flowers and musk, and the sweetest desert honey. "How about you come on my tongue a million times?"

———

JOLENE

She felt hot and cold at the same time, and prickles of goose-flesh blossomed on her arms. Her butt still stung from Zach's belt, but it was a good pain and reminded her of all the things she'd missed about being part of a couple.

A tiny, very dumb inner voice said she was cheating on Ben, but she pushed it down. Ben was gone, and he'd flat told her he didn't want her to be alone. Jolene would always miss him, but it was time to move forward. She was tired of being lonely. Tired of using her widowhood as a shield to avoid intimacy.

Maybe Zach was tired of being alone too. By his own choice, he'd missed out on everything she'd taken for granted for so long, not the least of which were her children. Ben was gone, but that didn't lessen what they'd shared.

Although still nervous about a potential new relation-ship, she decided Zach and Ben were both right. Maybe things wouldn't work out, but she'd never know unless she tried. Maybe it would end, and it would hurt.

But maybe it wouldn't.

Instead of going downtown like he'd promised, Zach kissed his way back up her stomach, then cupped her cheek. "You still with me, sweetheart?"

Jolene got her mind back on business, cursing herself for

letting her attention wander. "Yes, sorry. Like I said, it's been a long time."

Lowering his head, he kissed her so softly and gently it almost brought tears to her eyes. She blinked them back, but knew she was in serious danger of falling hard for this man.

With one last nip to her lower lip, he pulled away, then kissed his way across her belly, tracing her stretch marks with the tip of his tongue. She wanted to turn away or figure out how to hide the unsightly lines, but her hands seemed frozen above her head, as if his order had bound them as firmly as rope.

Every touch seemed purposely calculated to drive her mad. A soft brush of his lips across a needy nipple. The bite of his nails as he pinched the other. His warm weight between her legs as he worshipped her with mouth and fingers.

Slowly, ever so slowly, Zach drove all thought from her head until there was nothing but his unique scent of evergreen and citrus, his touch, and sweetly aching desire.

And only then did he move down her body to her center. The first tentative touch of his tongue on her wet folds made her hips jerk up to meet the glancing contact, and she whimpered as he held her still, large callused hands keeping her in place.

God help her, if he tried to edge her, she'd have to contemplate murder of a not-very-innocent man.

As if he'd heard her homicidal inner thoughts, Zach

chuckled, blowing a stream of cool air across her damp pussy. She cried out, the tease of cold against her hot core sending a shiver down her spine.

"Zach, please!"

He laughed again and eased her thighs over his broad shoulders. The new position lifted her hips and he took advantage, swiping his tongue from the rosebud of her anus all the way up to her clit.

"I love it when little girls beg." Without waiting for her to answer, he sucked the tender bundle of nerves into his mouth and lashed it firmly with the tip of his tongue.

Jolene's breath left her body in a whoosh and her vision went fuzzy and dark as she approached the precipice of a monumental climax. The fingers of his left hand bit into the flesh padding her hip, holding her still as he pushed two fingers into her needy pussy.

The scruff of his shadow beard abraded the delicate skin of her mound, but all she could think about was the decadent, silky glide of his fingers pumping in and out of her. Instead of giving her a reprieve, he curled his fingers inside her, putting pressure on her g-spot.

She clenched her muscles, gasping as the orgasm built deep inside, gathering strength like a thunderstorm over the desert.

"Beg me, little girl," he breathed against her core. "Beg me to let you come."

Crying out in pained pleasure, Jolene tried to catch her

breath enough to form words. "Daddy, please! I need you! I need... please!"

He turned his hand somehow, then pressed a thumb against her anus, the slick of her arousal easing the tight ring of muscle open. The dark penetration set her nerve endings alight with illicit pleasure. She wanted to touch him. Sink her fingers in his hair and hold him to her pussy. Yet his order still bound her hands above her head.

Babbled words escaped her lips, the nonsensical sounds making him pull her overstimulated clit into his mouth and suck hard. Without warning, the wave of pleasure crashed over her, drowning her in all-consuming bliss as it swept her away.

In an attempt to regain her senses, Jolene stared unseeing at the ceiling above her head, her vision blurred with tears. Her inner muscles clenched spasmodically, sending little aftershocks through her body. Despite that, she still felt unfulfilled. Incomplete in a way she couldn't explain, yet she wasn't sure she could ask for more.

He said nothing as he moved up her body. Focusing on his blue eyes, she wanted to break the silence between them, but had no idea what to say, nor was she sure she could come up with anything coherent.

His brows wrinkled into a frown and he stroked hair out of her face. "Honey, are you okay?"

Jolene swallowed hard and tried to get her throat working. Zach's thick cock brushed against her inner thigh, and she whimpered softly, trying to position her core under him. "More, Daddy," she rasped. "Give me more."

A smirk lit up his face and he stood just long enough to take off his boxer briefs, then knelt between her legs. Lifting her thigh, he positioned himself at her entrance. "I thought you'd never ask."

9

ZACH

At his age, performance anxiety shouldn't have been a thing. His oral game had been on point though, thank fuck. Watching Jolene come apart, tasting her sweetness, had been humbling, amazing, thrilling. He'd have happily eaten her pussy for hours, and the thought of her riding his face made him bite back a groan.

"Baby girl, I'm going to fuck you blind," he whispered, lowering his head to nibble the sweet spot below her ear.

Jolene wrapped her legs around his hips, crossing her ankles behind his back. "Daddy, now please. I need you inside me."

A dart of electric pleasure shot down his spine as her wet

core brushed against his cock and he wasted no time positioning himself at her entrance. Zach wasn't exactly a virgin, but the sensation of her heated channel welcoming him was like nothing he'd ever experienced.

It was like coming home.

Weirdly, Zach wished for additional arms. He wanted to touch her everywhere. Wrap her in an embrace and never let her go. Slowly, he rocked himself into her, slow and so damned deep it felt like he was touching her soul. She cried out, screamed his name as she clamped down on him.

It was too much, and it had been too long. Despite his desire to make love to Jolene forever, he couldn't hold the tempest boiling in his gut any longer. Lowering his head, he took her mouth in a deep kiss, swallowing her passionate cries as he stilled inside her.

The explosive climax dragged an animalistic roar from his throat and he shuddered, wrapping his arms around her as he tried to quiet his ragged, halting breaths. Rolling to the side, he pulled her into his arms, unwilling to give her even an inch of space.

Jolene hummed in contentment, nuzzling his chest. "Totally worth the wait, Daddy."

He chuckled at her softly muttered words, enjoying the slide of her body against his. "Let's rest for a few hours, baby. We'll hunt Jake down later and have him make supper for us."

"Mmm. We should ask him to make his *gigot a la cuillère.*

No idea what's in it, but I could eat that and the potatoes he serves with it every day."

"Lamb something." He nuzzled her hair and closed his eyes. "Grilled cheese and tomato soup?"

"My grandmother used to make Welsh rarebit with tomatoes on brown toast." She breathed out, then went quiet, obviously falling asleep.

He considered going outside to work on the cross he'd promised, but decided Jolene had the right idea. Closing his eyes, he relaxed and joined her for a long nap.

———

"Captain, wake up."

Zach blinked, then rolled over to glare at Mark. "Go away before you wake—" He stretched out an arm to make sure Jolene was still asleep, but found nothing but cold sheets. "What did you do with Jolene?"

"I was going to ask you the same question." Without warning, Mark grabbed his arm and pulled him up, then slammed him against the wall. "If you hurt her, I'm going to—"

"Cool your jets, War," Ryan said, walking in. "You know better than to think Zach did anything."

"Can I put pants on before you try to kick my ass?" Zach asked, pushing Mark aside. "Where's Jolene?"

"Her truck is gone, but all her stuff is still in her suite," Sean replied. "We were hoping you'd know."

"We were talking about what Jake would make for supper." Zach found his jeans and boxers by the side of the bed and put them on. "She wanted lamb and potatoes. We fell asleep after that. Did she send you a message? I didn't give her my number."

Ryan shook his head, then checked his phone. "No, sir." Wincing, he glanced at the mussed sheets. "Sorry, Captain."

He should have known better. What the hell had he been thinking to assume Jolene would want anything to do with him? Of course, she'd have bolted at the first opportunity after getting her itch scratched. Rubbing his face, he sighed.

"It's fine." Zach finished dressing, then strode from the room. "I'm going to get started on that St. Andrew's cross."

At least he'd gotten laid. He supposed that was better than nothing, but he thought he'd developed a connection with Jolene. Slamming the door behind him, he stomped to the pile of lumber and started hauling it outside. On his second trip, Sean appeared in front of him like a fucking whack-a-mole.

"Found her, Captain. I tracked her phone to Flagstaff Medical Center." He tapped his phone, then added, "Sending you the address. She's not answering my texts, but I'm wondering if she became a grandma a little earlier than she expected."

He sauntered away, leaving Zach feeling like an ass. She must have gotten the call while he'd been asleep and taken off without thinking about waking him. A wry smile crossed his lips as he left his work behind and strode to his rental car. Zach might not have kids of his own, but he had no trouble imagining Jolene breaking land speed records to meet her first grandchild.

His footsteps stalled as he reached his vehicle. Would she want him there? What business did he have crashing such a private family event? Steeling himself, he got into his car and fastened his seatbelt. Maybe he didn't belong, but he needed to be there for his baby girl.

A bit over an hour later, he reached the hospital and parked, then found the maternity ward. Zach wasn't sure why he was surprised to find it locked down. It wasn't as if he'd ever had reason to visit one. After reading the instructions posted next to the door, he pressed the buzzer.

An intercom crackled to life, and a woman's voice said, "Welcome to Flagstaff Medical Center. How can we assist you?"

Zach grimaced, realizing he didn't know Jolene's daughter's name. "I'm Zach Stratton. My friend Jolene Miller's daughter is having her baby, and I wanted to give Jolene my support. Is it okay if I wait out here?"

"Yes, sir. I'll pass your message along to the family."

"Thanks. I appreciate it."

The intercom clicked off, and Zach found a seat near the door. His stomach rumbled, and he winced when he glanced at the time. Jolene was probably hungry too, and he hadn't even thought of bringing her something to eat. Then again, she was probably too busy to think about food, and there was no guarantee she'd want him there at all.

Still, he needed to know for sure.

He found a bank of vending machines and grabbed a few candy bars, along with a couple of bottles of water. When he returned to his seat, a nurse was waiting. She wore bright pink scrubs and her long brown hair was pulled up in a messy pony tail.

"Mr. Stratton?" she asked.

"Yes, that's me."

"Great. The family has agreed to allow you in for a brief visit. I just need your driver's license, and we'll get you set up with a mask and ID bracelet. May I ask what your relationship is to the family?"

"I'm..." He paused a moment, trying to figure out how to explain to this woman that he'd just woken up from banging the family matriarch to unconsciousness and wanted to do it again for the rest of his life. "I'm Jolene's boyfriend," he finally said, knowing the word didn't come close to what he wanted with her.

Eyes twinkling with amusement, the nurse opened the door wider. "I kind of thought so. Mrs. Miller is blushing like crazy."

After presenting his ID, he was given a mask and a barcoded hospital bracelet, then shown to a large suite that looked like someone's bedroom. A young redhead, the spitting image of Jolene, was asleep in the hospital bed, curled up against a dark-haired young man, whom Zach assumed to be the father of the infant in Jolene's arms.

Seated in a rocker, she crooned softly, the mask covering the lower half of her face muffling the sound. The nurse held a finger to her lips, then left the room. Quietly, he made his way to the chair and crouched.

"Hey, baby girl," he whispered. "I see you got something there."

———

JOLENE

She'd been so afraid Zach wouldn't come. How could he have ignored her message for so long? After spilling her guts and all her secrets, she couldn't believe he'd just blown her off like that. Trying to control her irritation and hurt, she looked up, trying not to glare. "Where have you been?"

"You didn't tell anyone where you were going, sweetie. Sean had to track your phone, and we didn't know what had happened."

"I didn't have your number, so I sent Ryan a text. He was supposed to wake you." She frowned, then fished her phone from her pocket and winced when she saw the unsent text, along with several from Sean. She'd been so frantic to get to the hospital, she hadn't bothered actually sending it. "Whoops. I'm sorry."

She showed him the message she'd tried to send and he nodded, then asked, "Why didn't you wake me?" Moving her feet to the side, he sat on the edge of the ottoman and laid a hand on her knee.

"I tried. You were out cold, and I had to hurry, so I decided to let the boys try. They were supposed to tell you where I was, but seeing as how I was an idiot and didn't actually send the text..."

Shrugging, she tried for a smile, hoping she didn't look too much the fool. Thank God he didn't seem to notice how upset she'd been, or the overwhelming relief that must have been on her face.

"It's okay, baby girl. Daddy's here." Leaning close, he kissed her, then looked down at the infant in her arms. "Do I get an introduction?"

That single sentence made all the worry and hurt cramping her belly fade into warmth. Sitting in his lap would have made everything perfect, but her daughter's birthing suite wasn't the time or the place.

"Siobhan Lillian Gomez, meet your..." She gave him a cheeky grin, then added, "...Nana's new boy toy."

"Welcome to the family, little one. Your Nana was so

impatient to meet you, she's gone and gotten herself in trouble."

A pulse of shivery arousal darted through her core, making Jolene squeeze her thighs together. "We'll have to take care of that later."

Smirking, Zach leaned toward her, then cupped her jaw and kissed her. "Much later," he whispered against her lips. "After the dungeon is put together."

Jolene closed her eyes and let out a soft whimper of need. This totally wasn't the time for Zach to pull out his Daddy mojo. "Behave yourself," she finally said, once her brain came back online. "There are children present."

"You two are disgustingly cute," a tired feminine voice said from the bed. "Stop making out in front of my baby, or I'll tell Carrie on you."

"Cyndi! Manners!" Smiling inwardly, Jolene shook her head. Cyndi always did have a mouth on her.

Zach winked at Jolene, then stood and faced Cyndi, inclining his head. "I'm Zach Stratton. It's a pleasure to meet you."

"Cyndi Gomez." She nestled closer to Matty and closed her eyes. "This is my husband, Matteo. My sister Carrie won't make it until tomorrow. How long have you been seeing my mother?"

Matteo waved half-heartedly, then pulled Cyndi close. "We'll do the formal interrogation some other time," he said, sounding just as tired as Cyndi. "Until then, go to sleep."

A tear pricked Jolene's eye as she was reminded of her and Ben after Cyndi was born. They'd shared a bed while Ben's mother held baby Cyndi so they could sleep.

"Fine." Cyndi huffed out a breath, then leveled Zach with a beady stare. "Just to let you two crazy kids know, the woman in the suite next door is forty-three and delivered twins this morning. Siobhan doesn't need any more aunties or uncles."

"You don't say." Zach cocked his head, then gave Jolene a wicked smile. "I guess we'll have to be careful then."

Jolene blinked in surprise and her face got hot at Zach's knowing smirk. She hadn't once considered having another baby at her age, but shook the thought away. It was way too soon to be thinking about things like that, especially since she was positive Zach was teasing.

"I don't want to know. Both of you, go away and let us sleep." She reached over and slapped the call button.

The maternity nurse bustled in and gently took Siobhan, then placed her in a warming bassinet next to the bed. It was all Jolene could do to let the baby go, but Cyndi and Matteo needed their rest. Gently, she kissed Cyndi's cheek, then squeezed Matteo's shoulder.

"We'll be back tomorrow," she promised. "Congratulations, Mom and Dad."

Wrapping an arm around her waist, Zach led her outside. "Where are you parked?"

"Um..." Wincing, she rubbed her face, suddenly exhausted. "I'm sure my truck is probably somewhere in this lot."

"I see. Have you eaten?"

"Not since this morning, but I'm okay."

"Uh huh." Tightening his grip on her waist, he led her to a small sedan and opened the passenger door. "Get in. We'll get something to eat, then I'll take you home."

"But—"

"Get in, baby girl. You don't want me to spank you here in this parking lot, do you?"

"No, Daddy." She let him help her in and closed her eyes as he fastened the seatbelt over her hips. As much as she wanted to pretend she was strong enough to get herself home, she was more than happy to let Zach take care of her.

She still couldn't believe she'd been stupid enough not to send that text, and it was astonishing to know Zach had come looking for her.

After climbing in next to her, he took her hand. "Congratulations, Nana. I'm so thrilled for your blessing."

"Thanks." Leaning over, she rested her head on his shoulder. "My house is about twenty minutes away. If you could drop me off on your way back to Winslow, I'll get an Uber to the hospital tomorrow."

"Food first. After that, I'll be staying with you." He started the car, then had her put her address in the navigation system. As they got closer to her home, he pointed at a fast-food restaurant. "Burgers okay?"

"Yeah."

He went through the drive-through and she chose something at random from the menu. Although she thought she should be hungry, there were too many unspoken words between them to even think about food.

After parking in front of her small ranch, he helped her out, then held the food while she unlocked the door and opened it for him.

"Nice place," he murmured, following her into the kitchen.

"Thanks." She retrieved plates from the cupboard, then filled glasses with water while he laid out their food. "Zach, I owe you an apology, and also my thanks."

"Do you?" He sat, then poured ketchup on his plate and ate a French fry. "What for?"

"For leaving you like that. You must have thought I—"

"I actually did." He ate another fry. "The boys woke me up and demanded to know where you were. I figured you'd taken off because you didn't want to be around me."

"No! I would never do that!" She grimaced and picked at her food. "But I see how it must have looked, and I'm so sorry."

"Don't be." He took a huge bite of his burger, then chewed and swallowed. "We didn't have a chance to exchange phone numbers, and the only thing I'm irritated about is that you drove by yourself. Considering you don't know where you parked, I'm thinking you were in no fit shape to operate a vehicle. How many spanks should you get for that?"

"Five?"

Arching a brow, he nodded. "Okay, five, but only because you did actually type out a text, but forgot to hit send. How old are you?"

She blinked at the abrupt segue. "Forty-two."

"Mark was right. You're barely old enough to be a grandmother. You're actually only a few years older than Sean, so I'm guessing you are indeed firing live rounds, baby girl. I'd love to give you another ten for not considering a pregnancy might be possible, but I was right there with you and didn't stop it."

"But I..." She looked down at her barely-touched meal, realizing he was right. She'd been beyond careless. Sighing, she nodded. "You're right. As unlikely as it is, it's theoretically possible."

"We'll get you a pregnancy test in a few weeks. Eat your supper."

"Yes, Daddy." She ate an onion ring , but it tasted like cold sawdust. "What if I am? I'm sure I'm not, but what if—"

He set the last of his burger on his plate, then gazed at her. "Would you hate me if I told you I kind of hope you are?"

Swallowing hard, she nearly choked on the lump of

greasy onion. "No, but there is so much wrong with that statement, I can't even begin to unpack it."

"I know." He finished his food, then calmly wiped his hands. "My inner cave man is delighted with the idea of putting a baby in you. My wiser half reminds me I'd be collecting Social Security when he or she graduates from high school."

The incongruous comment made her burst into giggles. "I wouldn't be far behind you. Can you imagine how awkward that would be? Cyndi would kill me. Hers and mine would be Irish twins the hard way."

Eyes twinkling with amusement, he laughed with her, then sobered and reached for her hand. "The thing I most want is a chance. Maybe a baby between us isn't possible, but that doesn't mean we can't finish getting old together and skip right to the spoiling of grandchildren part."

He stood, then rounded the table to help her up. "So, what do you say? Want to take a chance on an old war horse put out to pasture?"

Standing in the house she'd owned for most of her adult life, Jolene stepped into Zach's arms and laid her head on his chest. The sensation was both familiar and strange, and her worries faded under his comforting touch.

She'd always believed in love at first sight. The minute she'd laid eyes on Ben, she'd told herself he would be her husband. Maybe she was older and wiser now. Maybe she and Zach had started off on the wrong foot.

But she no longer believed they were too old to have that second chance. Looking into his warm blue eyes, she said the first thing that popped into her head.

"Giddy-up, Daddy."

————

Are you ready to reserve your suite at Club Apocalypse? War's Peace is available wherever ebooks are sold.

ACKNOWLEDGMENTS

As always, my undying gratitude and love go to Engineer Hubby. Without your support and faith, I wouldn't be writing at all. Love you to the moon and back, baby.

———

Want to see what I'm up to next? Join my Renegades on Facebook. You can also sign up for my newsletter to receive a free short story delivered right to your inbox!

ABOUT RAISA GREYWOOD

USA TODAY BESTSELLING AUTHOR OF FILTHY SMUT, EMPTY NESTER, AND CAT SNUGGLER.

———

Raisa has worked as a teacher, an actuary (her husband called her a bookie—which isn't too far from the truth), mother, and scout leader. She's happily married to her husband of twenty-seven years, and is now enjoying semi-retirement writing the books she always wanted to read with kick-ass heroines and sexy, sexy men.

www.raisagreywood.com

f facebook.com/AuthorRaisaGreywood

instagram.com/raisagreywood

BB bookbub.com/authors/raisa-greywood

g goodreads.com/raisa_greywood

tiktok.com/@raisagreywood

Breaking Donatella

Bridgewater Brides

Their Wanted Bride

Cocky Hero Club

Sexy Scoundrel

Standalone Titles & Anthologies

Ladder 54: Five Firefighter Romances

Masters of the Castle: Witness Protection Program

Happily Never After (written with Sinistre Ange)

Demon Lust

Blood Lust

Made in the USA
Middletown, DE
06 September 2023

38123105R00068